TALES for HEADS

Published in paperback in 2021 by Sixth Element Publishing
on behalf of Nigel Northcott

Sixth Element Publishing
Arthur Robinson House
13-14 The Green
Billingham TS23 1EU
www.6epublishing.net

© Nigel Northcott 2021

ISBN 978-1-914170-08-9

British Library Cataloguing in Publication Data. A catalogue record for this book is available from the British Library.

All rights reserved. No part of this publication may be reproduced, stored in a retrieval system or transmitted, in any form or by any means, electronic, mechanical, photocopying, recording and/or otherwise without the prior written permission of the publishers. This book may not be lent, resold, hired out or disposed of by way of trade in any form, binding or cover other than that in which it is published without the prior written consent of the publishers.

Nigel Northcott asserts the moral right to be identified as the author of this work.

Printed in Great Britain.

This work is entirely a work of fiction. The names, characters, organisations, places, events and incidents portrayed are either products of the author's imagination or used in a fictitious manner. Any resemblance to actual persons, living or dead, or actual events is purely coincidental.

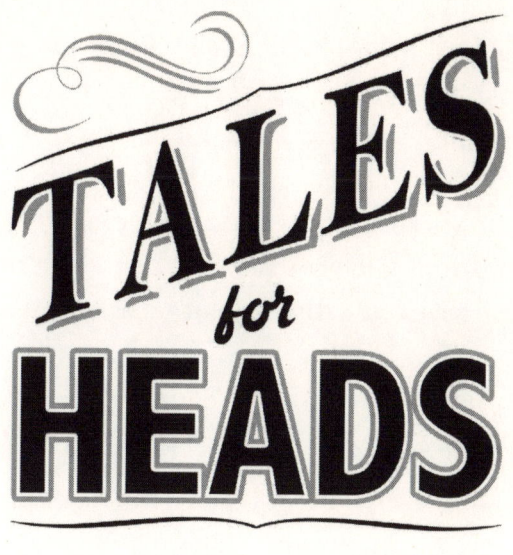

NIGEL NORTHCOTT

ABOUT THE AUTHOR

Nigel followed up his four O levels (GCSEs) by qualifying as a nurse and teacher and received a doctorate from Southampton University. As well as a career in nursing, education and management, he has also been a gardener, director of a homelessness charity, Buddhist chaplain and dad to two sons. He lives with his wife, the 'boys', their dog, chickens and canaries in Oxfordshire.

INTRODUCTION

Stories are the lifeblood of human culture and more particularly, storytelling has sharpened social thinking, encouraged cooperation and been at the centre of human creativity and learning. In forty years as an educator, I have found stories a helpful way to explain, illustrate and explore points and issues. These one-hundred-and-one stories are a blend, and whilst none are blue, they are: old, new and borrowed. Several are stories that I have heard or been told and for which there may be one or more 'original' sources or that ubiquitous pen of tradition. What is common to the stories is the element of a moral, a meaning or lesson to be learnt and I hope pleasure in reading them. I, of course, offer an invitation to you… if on reading this you recall a story that is like those here, please contact me and maybe a second book will emerge.

CONTENTS

1 Have you put the cat out?... 1
2 Cooking frogs!... 3
3 Two men and a donkey.. 4
4 Albus and the fruit.. 6
5 Who gives you wisdom?... 8
6 At the cross roads 10
7 Starfish... 12
8 The stone cutter 13
9 The unlucky stork 15
10 The abbot and the tea cup 17
11 Bullock cart racing.. 19
12 The splendid mango... 22
13 The three sons.. 24
14 The girl and the ogre... 26
15 The fox and the lion... 29
16 The sandwich 31
17 The apple seed 33
18 The king's heir.. 35
19 The salt!... 37
20 Obsessed with diamonds..................................... 39

21 Roast sausages	41
22 The crow	43
23 The black stallion	45
24 Bad habits	47
25 The blue spot	49
26 Peace of mind	51
27 The lawn	53
28 Bread and cheese	55
29 The coffin	57
30 The lost horse	59
31 The dishonest student	61
32 The teapot	63
33 The frog and the goldfish	65
34 The water bearer	67
35 The traveller	69
36 Two rabbits	70
37 The mighty emperor	72
38 The rat and the cat	74
39 The bandit and the teacher	76
40 Oysters	78
41 The chillies	80
42 The stall holders	82
43 The horizon	84

44 Sharpen the saw	86
45 The vicar and the policeman	88
46 The X-ray!	91
47 The worry tree	93
48 The splendid meal	95
49 The man and the tiger	97
50 The man and his dog	99
51 The pizza	101
52 The river crossing	103
53 It's a Marmite thing!	105
54 What to be good at	107
55 The rotten apple	110
56 Bad students, good teacher!	112
57 The limpet	114
58 The fisherman	116
59 The jigsaw	118
60 Flies or bees	120
61 Change	122
62 Which way do you face?	124
63 The sat nav	126
64 Can a donkey be a cow?	128
65 Two envelopes	130
66 The concentration camp	132

67 The old violin 134
68 The golden Buddha 136
69 Pandora's box 138
70 The manager 140
71 The pot plants 142
72 Tulip bulbs 144
73 The old lion 146
74 What to learn 148
75 The tribal mask 151
76 The old bear 153
77 Blame the tools! 155
78 The strange teacher 157
79 Questions! 160
80 The badminton match 162
81 Help my son! 164
82 The king 166
83 Three sons 168
84 The crows and the snake ... 170
85 The ladle 172
86 Breath 174
87 Elephant rope 176
88 Gold coins 178
89 The pebbles and debt 180

90 The farmer's butter	182
91 The weight of water	184
92 The exam	186
93 Sweets and marbles	188
94 The three sons	190
95 Where's your furniture?	192
96 The old car	194
97 Move the mug	196
98 The scissors and the axe	198
99 The next life	200
100 The men at lunch	202
101 The chess game	204

1 HAVE YOU PUT THE CAT OUT?

Tom had approached the abbot of a monastery and asked if he might stay there with a view to joining the holy order. He was invited to stay for a week to see if it worked out for him and the order. After that time, matters would be reviewed. He slept fitfully that first night and was still tired at 4.30am when the bell rang for the first meditation sitting of the day. Tom was almost the last to enter the small shrine room and he was about to sit down when the abbot addressed him.

"Welcome Tom, it is good to have you with us and I trust you will find your stay here helpful and beneficial. Before you sit could I ask you to check that the cat has been put out of the kitchen? She'll get into everything whilst we are sitting if we leave her there."

Tom knew obedience was an important aspect of community life and quickly got up and left the shrine room and went to the kitchen at the other side of the house and checked for the cat. There was no sign of a cat and Tom made sure the windows were all closed and the door shut behind him before he returned and took his place in the shrine room. Tom sat in silence for around forty minutes, at the end of which time a bell was rung and he was asked by the abbot to go and help organise breakfast for the order. Tom joined one of the order members in the kitchen and was asked to make a large pan of porridge, whilst his associate sorted out bowls, spoons and made a big pot of tea.

"How long have you had the cat and what colour is it?" Tom enquired. He was keen to know more about this mischievous cat and was surprised when the associate said, "We don't have a cat. I've been here nine years and have never seen a cat!"

Tom was puzzled by this and began to question whether in his half-awake state at 5am he had misheard the abbot or maybe it was his obedience that was being tested! "We did have one here many years ago, it was a tabby and on occasions it got into the kitchen and made a mess. So, the abbot decreed that before we sat in the shrine, one of the order should check that the cat was not in the kitchen and I guess we've done that ever since!"

Like so many of us, the order had got into a habit years ago and despite it obviously no longer being of need or value had stuck with it. Maybe we should all look over our lives to see what habits we have hung onto despite them no longer being of value.

2 COOKING FROGS!

If you take a saucepan of water and bring it to the boil and throw in a live frog – surprise, surprise… it will jump straight out. However, if you put a frog in pan of cold water and place it on the heat, the frog will stay put as the water temperature rises until eventually it will be boiled alive!

Are we that second frog, failing to notice that we are being boiled alive? For example, do we realise the damage to our lungs by smoking until they are seriously damaged, or the long-term effect stress is having on us when we first feel under pressure. We might have or be putting on weight as a result of overeating or eating too much junk food. Or maybe we don't get enough exercise? It is often only when our life habits and behaviours have begun to 'boil' us alive that we realise we need to act and maybe by then it is too late. We rarely get dropped straight into boiling water and if we did, we would soon jump out! It is never too late to seek help if we feel we are being boiled alive, but maybe we should think about the consequences of our actions in the long term in order that we avoid be boiled alive.

3 TWO MEN AND A DONKEY

A merchant called his son one day and told him they should go to the market that morning. They loaded up their donkey with goods and produce to sell and set off to walk to the town. After a few miles they caught up with a neighbour who was walking into the town. "Well, there's a thing, you have a fine donkey and yet you walk. A man of your years should rest his legs," said the neighbour.

The merchant thought this through and decided indeed he should ride, so he climbed onto the animal's back and they set off once more. After a few more miles, they caught up with another neighbour who they exchanged greetings with.

"Well, there's a thing, you ride in comfort and make your young son walk. You lazy thing," said the neighbour.

The man felt guilty and insisted his son swap places with him and once more they set off, this time with the son riding. After a few more miles, they caught up with another neighbour who they exchanged greetings with.

"Well, there's a thing, you have a fine donkey and yet you walk, father. That beast could surely carry you both. You should make the animal work," said the neighbour.

The man agreed the animal was built to work and carry so he climbed up behind his son and once more they set off with them both riding. After a few more miles they caught up with another neighbour who they exchanged greetings with.

"Well, there's a thing, you two weighing that poor animal down. How could you be so cruel?"

The merchant thought carefully about this comment and minutes later the two entered the market square to hoots of laughter from the crowd as they struggled between them to carry the donkey!

Sometimes it seems that whatever you do you won't please everyone!

4 ALBUS AND THE FRUIT

Albus lived in a country where no fruit trees grew, but he had many hours reading and often came across references to fruit trees and indeed fruit. The descriptions encouraged him to make a journey to find and experience fruit for himself. He sailed for many days and eventually landed in a country far from his own. He asked the local fishermen where he might find fruit. They gave him directions and after walking for three days he arrived at a hillside pasture where there was a large apple orchard. It was spring and all the trees were covered in glorious pink blossom. Albus entered the orchard and pulled off a blossom and put it in his mouth. The blossom had little flavour and a rather fluffy texture and he quickly spat it out. He tried blossom from several trees and each time spat out the flowers, dissatisfied with their taste and texture. He had to admit the blossom looked fine but did not meet his expectations of fruit from descriptions he had read in books. He left the orchard and returned to his home country, where he told his villagers that fruit was rather overrated and he couldn't see how or why authors had praised it so much. Albus was not able to recognise the difference between the spring blossom and the fruit that would follow later in the year; he never realised that he had not experienced what he was looking for. We will all set out in life in search of experiences that others have let us know about, but unless we know exactly what the experience is like we may not know when or if we have found it!

5 WHO GIVES YOU WISDOM?

There was once a young man keen to become wise and to improve himself; so, he went one day to the market where he was told he might find someone to help him. He spoke to many people that day and got all manner of advice and ideas about how to become wise and how he might better himself. As the day drew to a close, he feared he knew a great deal but was not sure what advice was helpful and what he should ignore. He was sitting on the steps of the market square when an elderly woman approached him asking why he seemed so troubled. He explained that he had hoped that he would know what he should do to become wise but that he had been told so much he was now confused. The old woman handed him a ring and told him to ask several market stall holders how much they would give him for it. He was soon back at her feet and reported that they had offered as little as one hundred silver pieces and as much as three hundred.

"Now go and ask the jeweller in his shop by the clock tower," she commanded.

"Well, that is strange. He offered me three thousand silver pieces," he reported.

"When you want advice, pay heed to who you ask; the stall holders merely wished to take advantage of your ignorance but the jeweller knew his trade and what the ring was truly worth."

From that day forth the man sought out only the finest teachers and ignored the freely offered ramblings of his companions. Think of where you get advice and guidance from. Is the person really wise and knowledgeable?

6 AT THE CROSS ROADS

An elderly woman sat at a crossing point on the road that came down from the hills to a town below in the valley. As she sat, a traveller approached her looking tired and weary.

"What is it like in the town below?" he asked of her.

"Tell me," she replied, "what was it like where you have come from?"

"Oh, don't ask, it was dreadful; full of thieves, liars and cheats and I had a terrible time."

"Well, that, my friend, is as it is in the town below!" she responded.

Disheartened, the traveller turned and set off on the high road away from the valley. A few minutes later, another traveller approached her looking tired and weary. He smiled at her and enquired, "Good day, could you tell me what it is like in the town below."

"Tell me", she replied, "what was it like where you have come from?"

"It was delightful, a land of opportunity and good people, but I got itchy feet and needed to move on."

"Well, that, my friend, is as it is in the town below!"

He thanked the lady and set off along the road to the town below in the valley.

Interesting how she gave such different answers to the same question from the two travellers, but then she knew what it was like in the town below and she also knew much of how you find a place depends upon you and your attitudes. The previous town had been a success for the second traveller and this probably says as much about him as it does about the town.

How do you approach situations and new opportunities? Do you expect failure or are you more of a bottle half full person? Do you have that attitude that sees new experiences as opportunities and does your positive attitude help ensure you make and get the most of new situations? Or are you like the first traveller – it's always been grim for you where you've been so far. Maybe it's you! It is odd that you can put two individuals in a situation and each will report very differently about what it was like. Years ago, I worked in a small industrial unit and on my first day an existing member of staff told me it was a terrible place to work and he had hated it from day one and couldn't wait to leave to any other job. I stayed two years and enjoyed every minute and gained a great deal from the experience – he left a few weeks after I started and was soon reporting his new job was grim as well.

7 STARFISH

Two people were walking along a beach where millions of starfish had been washed up by the high tide and a storm at sea. The poor animals were clearly struggling as the sun came up and they began to dry out. As they walked along the shore, they took care not to tread on the animals, but it was not easy as there were so many stranded out of the water. Every so often the first person picked up a starfish and threw it back into the sea.

"You're wasting your time… there are so many animals washed up," said the second, clearly concerned at the futility of his friend's efforts.

"I am not wasting my time for those that I throw back!" came the reply.

We all sometimes find ourselves in situations where there appears to be so much to do. How do you respond? Are you like the first person that at least does what they can to help or do you stand there and give up in the face of so much to do? In our lives we may face situations where there seems to be so much to do. Do you get started on the list doing what you can? Or in the face of so much to do, do you just give up?

8 THE STONE CUTTER

Once a stone cutter sat chipping away at a stone that was to become a sculpture in the local park. The cutter regretted his existence and felt he wanted to be more influential and important. As he worked, he sang a song. "My pointless life will soon be done, all I've done is chip at stone…"

As he sang, he was startled to see a vision of a spirit appear in front of him. The spirit asked him why was he was so despondent and he explained he felt worthless and unimportant. He said that if he was, say the sun, he could control everything. He would decide how hot the world was, how fast crops would grow and what people would be able to do. The spirit clapped its hands and the man found himself in the sky as the sun. He at last felt good and powerful.

But his joy was short-lived. A cloud blew in front of him, blocking out his rays from reaching the earth and once more his heart filled with sorrow and he felt useless. Once more he sang the song and again the spirit reappeared. He explained how the cloud had stopped him and that if he was a cloud, he too could block the sun! The spirit clapped its hands again and he turned into a cloud where he sat blocking the sun!

Then all changed – the wind blew and he found himself scudding across the sky and once again his heart filled with sorrow and he felt useless. Once more he sang the song and again the spirit reappeared. He explained how the wind had stopped him and that if he was the wind, he too could blow the clouds around! The spirit clapped its hands again and he turned into the wind where he merrily blew the clouds about and he even blew the leaves and dust on the earth to annoy the people below.

But his joy was short-lived. As hard as he blew, a big rock refused to budge and the people even sheltered behind it. Once more his heart filled with sorrow and he felt useless. Once more he sang the song and again the spirit reappeared. He explained how the rock had resisted him and he wished to be a rock blocking the wind. The spirit clapped its hands again and he turned into a rock where he sat resisting the wind and even blocking out the sunlight!

But his joy was short-lived. He became aware of a sensation at his base… a man was chipping away at him and he was growing smaller with each hit. Once more his heart filled with sorrow and he felt useless. Once more he sang the song and again the spirit reappeared. He explained how the man was chipping away at him and that if he was that man he too could chip away at the rock! The sprit clapped its hands again and he turned into the man making the sculpture!

Maybe we would do better to accept what and who we are and work to improve ourselves rather than think that by being something or someone else we might succeed!

9 THE UNLUCKY STORK

There was once a handsome grey stork who spent his days hunting for small fish, crustaceans and bugs in the wetlands around a local farm. He had stayed in the location throughout the winter and had spent most days with a flock of cranes that only ate vegetation, leaving all the creepy crawlies to him. He had grown well and each day feasted alongside the cranes who, although rather noisy, provided safety in numbers. One afternoon, he was at the edge of the pond when he heard a muffled bang and found himself inside a big net with many of his newfound crane friends. He then saw the farmer and his workers approach with sticks and one by one hit the cranes on the head to dispatch them – they had eaten all the farmer's crops that he was growing around the pond and wetlands. The stork began to worry and tried to convince himself the farmer would notice he was a stork and was not one of the greedy cranes that had eaten all the crops. He even protested to the cranes but it was to no avail… eventually the farmer grabbed him by the neck and he feared his end was nigh! Just as the stick was about to hit his head, the farmer slipped in the mud and lost his grip and the stork found himself free. He beat his wings furiously and was soon high above the pond and the farm and was safe.

He flew towards the hills behind the farm and with

tired wings from his escape he landed in a tall pine tree. In the tree sat a wise old owl who greeted him with a gentle hoot! He told the owl of his lucky escape and the owl listened carefully before saying,

"Well, that should teach you to choose your company more carefully. There is no doubt you meant the farmer no harm – indeed you were doing him a favour – but mixing in such unsavoury company as cranes was not wise!"

A lesson to us all to choose carefully who we associate with. I recall my when my sister was at secondary school, our dad came home saying, "The school says she's very bright but keeps bad company and no good will come of her mixing with that sort!"

10 THE ABBOT AND THE TEA CUP

There was once a man whose life seemed to be going all wrong and who, in desperation, decided to seek the advice of a holy man who lived at the local monastery. He knocked at the door and a young monk greeted him and asked his business. He told the monk that he wanted to know the secret of a happy and contented life and to escape the misery he was currently experiencing. The young monk called upon the abbot, who as the leader of the community, was the best person to help, and the man soon found himself in the presence of the much older monk who was sitting at a table. He was invited to sit with the abbot who immediately asked if he would like some tea. He accepted this hospitality and sat quietly looking at the calm focused face of the abbot.

The young monk returned with a tray of tea; a big pale blue teapot and two pale blue mugs upon a wooden tray. No sooner than the tray had been placed upon the table than the abbot began pouring tea into the first cup. The cup soon filled but the abbot continued to pour and soon the tray was awash with tea and, not long after, the tea began spilling onto the table and running off onto the floor. The man was startled and pointed out to the abbot that the tea was overflowing onto the floor. The elderly monk stopped pouring. He sat quietly for a few minutes before saying, "You come to me seeking wisdom, wanting to know how to get the best out of your life, yet your head, like the tea tray, is already overflowing. What you must first do is empty your mind. Only then can you hear my words of wisdom that will change your fortune."

Like so many of us, our heads are so full of nonsense and ideas that do not help, that we are not receptive to wisdom that we might come across or might be offered. Remember, it is our thoughts, habits, beliefs and actions that have led us to where we are today and if this is not the best place then we must open our minds to new ideas, options and possibilities. Like an umbrella, the human mind works best when it is open!

11 BULLOCK CART RACING

There was once a farmer who kept a prize bullock to help him plough his fields. The crops, however, had not grown well that year and he was facing ruin. He was fearful that he would not be able to feed his family as winter approached and was not sure what he should do. He went that morning, as he did every week, to the market in town and by selling the last of his stored crops, he was able to buy supplies for his family. He then noticed a sign in the market advertising a bullock cart race with a first prize that would see him through the winter and beyond. He decided that he would use his last savings to enter the race. He had faith that his bullock was strong and fast.

The day of the races soon came and he rode with his young son to the town to take part. There were five heats and the cart that came first in each heat would be in the final, and the winner of the final would take home the prize. He eagerly entered the first heat and indeed his bullock was strong and fast and he easily won. The finals were between seven farmers and their bullocks with the last two home in the first two matches being eliminated. The grand final would between the three remaining entrants.

In the first of these matches, the farmer was in the lead until close to the end – when to his surprise a cart passed him. Fearing he might get eliminated, he leant over his beast and hit it on the rump with his stick, but to no avail… another cart passed him and he came third! In the second heat once again, he pulled out at the front and, nearing the end, a cart passed him. Once again, he used his stick and again another cart passed him. He was third, but with a place in the grand finale. But how could he win? He had been beaten twice already by the same two carts. He was in despair. He had gambled all his money on winning and now faced defeat.

As he prepared his bullock and cart at the start of the last race, his young son told him he would take the reins. He was much lighter than the farmer and this might help. Desperate to try anything, the farmer agreed and the young boy took control in the final race. As before, the cart pulled ahead and as the race entered its final stages the two other carts drew close and were about to overtake. The farmer shouted to his son to use the stick to encourage the beast. Buy the boy left it at his side and risking his life, he left the seat and laid across the animal's back. The bullock responded and surged forward, crossing the line first. As soon as they crossed the line, the farmer ran forward to claim his prize and as soon as he had the money the boy asked for one small silver coin. The farmer gave it to the boy as his share of the winnings and the boy ran off to the market to spend it.

The farmer was surprised to see his son run back carrying a large turnip in his hands. What a strange reward the boy had chosen for helping them win! The boy took his knife and cut into the vegetable and placed all the pieces on the ground for the bullock!

That day the farmer learnt an important lesson from his son – kindness makes a better motivator than punishment. The boy had leant forward in the final race and offered the bullock the reward of that giant turnip and it responded. The father had tried beating the beast to respond!

How might every aspect of our lives change if there was greater emphasis on rewarding good conduct and less on punishing bad!

12 THE SPLENDID MANGO

There was once a tree in a wood that grew the most glorious mangoes on it. The other mango trees in the wood were much smaller and had much smaller mangoes that were not as sweet, not as juicy and not as big. As the trees grew towards the end of the year and the fruit began to swell, the tree started to brag. It told the other trees they were wasting their time… their fruit would be small and sour and dry. The tree told them their fruit would be useless and they would do well not to bother growing and they all felt unhappy and demoralised.

As the season ended, the fruit was ripe and ready to eat and the villagers came to pick it. They saw the fruit on the smaller trees and picked it and were quite happy. The big tree couldn't believe it – the stupid villagers happy with such small inferior fruit. The tree called to the forest monkeys and told them how stupid he thought the people were and the monkeys joined in the jeering and threw the big juicy mangoes at the people below. The villagers looked up and saw the tree standing above all the others and realised it had superior fruit. They fetched ladders and sticks and baskets and were soon amongst the branches grabbing the fruit. After an hour of frenzied activity, the tree was in a right state… many branches had been broken off and most of the leaves pulled off as the people clambered to get all the splendid mangoes. As the night fell and the people retreated to the village, the tree stood forlorn and distraught.

"Look what has happened to me," said the tree. "I look such a mess. It will take all year to recover."

"Had you been less boastful and not 'so much better' than the rest of us, you'd have been fine," said a small mango tree nearby.

We should take care when we put our head above the parapet and get superior to others. Pride comes before a fall. Being so boastful and claiming to be so much better than the others, the tree was singled out for attention and suffered. Better to humbly be one of the crowd and keep your head down.

13 THE THREE SONS

There was once a king who had grown old and tired and sensed his days were numbered. He had three sons – each worthy of ruling after the old king, and he was not sure which should be given the honour. He told the three sons to go to the top of the nearby mountain and bring back the most important thing that they came across on that journey. The three sons set off eagerly, keen to return with the most important thing.

The first son returned later that day with a big sack of flints, telling his father that he had found a source of the best flints from which the people could make fire, create axe heads and arrow heads; to keep warm as well as defend themselves. The king was pleased and very impressed.

The second son came back with a bundle of dry wood. He had found an endless supply of quality wood which the people could use to keep warm and to make tools, plates and cups as well as build homes. The king was delighted and very impressed.

His third son came back saying the mountain top was barren and there was nothing there worth bringing back. However, from the top, he had seen the view of the lands far from the castle where there were plains full of animals, forests full of trees and lakes and rivers full of fish. The land was fertile and welcoming and the son said they would do well to travel there to enrich the lives of the people. He could not wait to set off and explore the lands.

The old king embraced his third son and said, whilst his first two sons had bought back worthy finds, his third son had bought back something worth so much more… vision. Not only had he seen potential of the lands beyond, but also, he had brought back a desire to go there to enrich the people!

What is your vision? Where are you going in life? We all have a past and maybe that past is not something we feel is our best. What matters more is our future. Where will our vision take us?

14 THE GIRL AND THE OGRE

In all the best children's stories there is an ogre and I am sure I can stretch you to read a 'fairy story'.

The village was a peaceful place to live and all the villagers enjoyed life and lived long and happy lives until one autumn evening an ogre turned up. The ogre had moved into the district as he had heard life was good, crops grew well and the people were all well fed and 'juicy'! (Juicy people taste good – not too much fat and plenty of protein!). He marched into the village square and called the people to attention; he was three times the size of the strongest warrior in the village and had purple skin and a long ginger beard. He bellowed at the top of his voice, causing a foul air to swirl around the village. He had very stinky breath! He told the people he had moved into the cave in the hills above the village and each day the people must bring him a wheelbarrow of food and each month a juicy villager to roast on his fire. If they failed, he would come to the village and squash a house each day until his demands were met and to prove his point he jumped on a house and flattened it!

The leaders of the village got together and decided they should agree to his demands and deliver the food, but also to challenge him and try and drive him away. They chose their best warrior to confront the ogre and take his longest spear to dispatch the creature.

The warrior went boldly to the cave and called to the ogre who came to the door asking why he was being disturbed. The warrior told the ogre to leave or he would impale him on his spear. The ogre laughed out loud and the warrior threw his spear at the ogre's heart. The ogre caught it, snapped it like a twig and sent the warrior running from the splinters.

The next day, the leaders of the village chose their best axe man to confront the ogre and take his largest axe to dispatch the creature. The warrior went boldly to the cave and called to the ogre who came to the door asking why he was being disturbed. The warrior told the ogre to leave or he would split his head with the axe. The ogre laughed out loud and the warrior threw his axe at the ogre's head. The ogre caught the axe and used it to trim his beard before throwing it back, sending the axe man running.

The next day, unbeknownst to the villagers, a young girl from the village set off to the cave and half an hour later they were all woken by the ogre's terrible thundering footsteps. But as they listened, they realised he was walking away from the district and not towards their homes and he was muttering under his breath, "I'm glad I know that – it would have been a disaster!"

When the young girl returned to the village, the people asked her what had happened. She told them the ogre was leaving! She had told him that he was risking his own life because the flesh of the villagers was poisonous which explained why there were no tigers living nearby. She told him the tigers had all died eating the poisonous people.

Little did the ogre know there had never been any tigers anywhere near the village.

We all too often try using our might and force to solve difficulties. Success is more likely if, like the young girl, we try using our heads... thinking our way out of trouble.

15 THE FOX AND THE LION

A man wandered into a clearing in the forest and noticed a fox lying under a bush at the far side. He stopped and carefully inched his way around the clearing until he had a good view. He was about to move even closer when he heard the low roar of a lion. Quickly he climbed a tree and waited until the lion came into the clearing, dragging a partly eaten deer behind it. He watched in amazement as the lion dragged its quarry over to the fox and dropped it at the fox's feet. The lion lay down as the fox greedily tore at the meat, filling its belly. Once full, the fox ignored the deer, and the lion took the remains away into the forest. The next day the man came to the same clearing and once more was amazed to see the fox still under the bush. It was clearly injured and unable to move away, and he was again amazed when the lion reappeared, dragging a plump jungle fowl that he laid at the fox's feet. The fox once again filled its belly and the man marvelled that the Almighty had provided for the lame fox.

The next day, the man went to the market steps and sat and waited... surely the Almighty would ensure he was fed! Each day he came and it was on the fourth day that he called out, "Almighty, I see you feed the fox. I have had nothing in four days!"

He was startled to hear a voice reply. "What troubles you?" it asked.

"I saw your example of the lion and fox, and I have been here four days yet no one has bought me as much as a crumb!"

"Ah, yes," said the Almighty. "I did ensure you saw my creatures in the forest."

"So why have you not fed me as you ensured the fox was fed?"

"I had hoped you might follow the example of the lion rather than follow the example of the fox!"

To what extent do we sit and wait for things to come to us? Maybe we should be more like the lion, providing for others.

16 THE SANDWICH

Late one afternoon, a business man was about to leave his office when he noticed an uneaten sandwich in the drawer of his desk. Fearing it might go off, he picked it up and took it with him. As he crossed the car park to his car, he thought of the special bottle of wine he was having that night with his steak dinner and, as he thought about the feast he was going home to, he saw a beggar. He placed the sandwich on the beggar's blanket and felt good that rather than it go in the bin, the sandwich would help keep hunger at bay for the beggar.

That night the man dreamed he was away on a business trip with his senior partners at an exclusive restaurant. Everyone had placed their orders, the wine was flowing and he was looking forward to a splendid evening of wining and dining. The food began to arrive... lobster, venison, pâté, T-bone steak and champagne, to the evident delight of his companions.

Then his order arrived. The waiter paced a small curled up sandwich in front of him.

"What's this?" he demanded. "This is supposed to be the best restaurant in the city and this is not what I ordered," be bellowed.

"Restaurant? Oh no, sir, this is not a restaurant, you are mistaken... this is heaven! And we can only serve you what you sent ahead whilst on earth. When I looked under your name, all that I could find was this small stale sandwich!"

If you are putting little into life, don't expect to get too much back! Whether you believe in a life after death or not matters little, for even day to day if you only give little, you cannot expect to get much in return.

17 THE APPLE SEED

There was once a man condemned to be hanged for stealing a loaf of bread. The king had made the decree to make an example of the man: it would serve as a lesson to others that dishonesty would not be tolerated. As the man was about to be taken to be executed, he was asked if he had any last words.

"Yes, I wish to tell your majesty that I have a gift handed down through many generations that I can plant an apple seed in such a way that the tree grows immediately and will be covered in splendid apples in minutes. It would be such a waste if the secret died with me."

The king agreed and asked for the secret. The man said he could only pass it to someone who had never been dishonest. Indeed, he could no longer plant a seed himself as he had taken food to feed his hungry family.

The king told his chancellor to plant the seed, but the man was clearly uneasy and said he regretted he had once kept something that did not belong to him. So, the king told his chief adviser to plant it, but he was also very uneasy and told the king he could not as he had once had a brief affair with a serving woman. The two ministers turned to the king and said that he should plant it as he was the only person who had not been dishonest. The king hesitated and his face went red as he told them that even this day, he had told his wife she looked splendid in a dress she had vainly squeezed herself into that actually looked dreadful.

"So even the most powerful men in the land cannot plant the seed through their dishonesty," the condemned man said. "I merely stole enough food to ensure my children did not starve."

The king realised he had been harsh and pardoned the man.

First, we should not look to condemn others for their dishonesty or misdemeanours, given we have all fallen short of the mark. And given that we have all done wrong or been unskilful, maybe we should each be looking for ways to put those wrongs right.

18 THE KING'S HEIR

The king was growing old and, as he had no children, he had no one to pass on his throne to, so he decreed that anyone could apply to be the next king as long as they were kind of heart. At the end of the month the candidates were invited to present themselves to the royal palace to be considered. Throughout the land people prepared themselves with the finest outfits. Even a young peasant boy worked hard all month to buy new clothes so that he might present himself; he would stand no chance in the rags he usually wore!

As the day approached, the peasant boy made his way to the castle and on the road, he came across a beggar. The man was shivering with cold and looked so forlorn, the peasant boy gave him the clothes he had worked hard to buy. Having given away his fine clothes, the peasant boy was left with his rags, but having come so far, he continued to the palace; after all he had never been inside the castle, let alone the palace. The guards laughed at him in his rags and teased him that he might get a job as a cleaner but not as the next king!

At last, the boy found himself in a great hall with all the candidates and he felt rather uneasy in his rags and rather than be appointed the king's adopted son, he did rather expect to be thrown out or offered a job cleaning! The king came down from the platform at the end of the great hall and walked amongst the candidates, peering carefully at each one. He suddenly stopped in the middle of all the candidates and thrust his royal mace upon the ground.

"I thank you all for coming today; many of you have come a long way and you have all made such an effort." The king stopped speaking, turned to the peasant boy who was standing behind him then knelt down and embraced the boy. "Welcome, my son," he exclaimed.

It was then the boy noticed the king was wearing the clothes that he had given to the roadside beggar that morning… the king had obviously set himself at the roadside to see who was coming to claim the throne. It is by our deeds and actions that we are judged. We might have fine clothes and be immaculately turned out, but what really shows us to be of good heart is what we do!

19 THE SALT!

Theo sat with his head in his hands. "I am so unworthy. My life is a mess. I have made so many mistakes."

Alexis, his lifelong friend, tried to console him but however hard he tried, Theo continued to put himself down, saying he was a failure and useless. Alexis suggested they go and speak to the wise hermit who lived by the lake. Together they walked to the hut where the hermit lived, with Theo protesting there was no point, he was beyond help.

The old man greeted them and soon Theo was telling him of all his failings, but the old man stopped him by offering to make tea for them all. Soon, a big brown teapot and three mugs sat on the small table and the hermit poured the tea. Theo was about to sip his tea when the hermit stopped him and said he needed to add a special herbal mixture that would help him. The hermit took a spoonful of the brownish crystals from the bowl on the table and stirred it into Theo's tea. Theo then tasted the tea and quickly pulled the cup from his mouth, protesting that the tea tasted salty. The hermit took the bowl of crystals and beckoned to the two men to follow him. He walked slowly to the edge of the lake where he bent down and stirred a spoonful of the crystals into the lake with his walking stick! He then bent down and took a handful of the water from the lake, tasted it and indicated the two men should copy him. Theo tasted the water. It was fresh and clear and had a slightly peaty taste but it was refreshing and pleasant to taste. The old man smiled and together they walked back to his cottage. The old man entered first and once inside he poured a fresh cup of tea for Theo and sat smiling at the two men!

After several minutes and after each man had drunk his tea, the old man spoke, telling Theo he must become more like the lake and less like the cup! Yes, indeed he had done unwise things and some of his actions were unskilful and some had been failures, but he should consider these shortcomings in the light of all he had done that was wise, helpful and skilful.

If we have only done a few good deeds, then, like the salt in the small cup, the taste of salt will be overwhelming, but we should dilute any shortcomings with a whole lake of good deeds. In many traditions there is talk of balancing good and skilful deeds against those that are without merit! If, however, you have only a 'cupful' of good deeds, you may never dilute the taste of your unskilful actions. Get that lake of good deeds full up so any unskilful actions are well and truly diluted.

20 OBSESSED WITH DIAMONDS

There was once a woman who was obsessed with diamonds. She was however not at all rich and even after saving for many years could only afford a pair of very small insignificant earrings that had small diamonds in them. She vowed to take on extra work to raise more money until she had three jobs, working from six in the morning until nine at night and at weekends. After many more years she still had not managed to save enough to buy the jewels she so desired. In desperation she went to the local money lender and sold her earrings and used the money to gamble with. She tried bingo, horse racing and even the national lottery, but all she did was lose money until she had nothing left.

She woke every morning tearful that, not only had she not got the jewels she so desired, she had now lost the earrings she so much loved and would walk past the money lender's window just to look at them. She would never realise her dream to have jewels and she feared she may never get her earrings back.

In desperation, late one morning she went to the jeweller's shop and asked to see a tray of his finest diamond jewellery so she might at least see and maybe touch the jewels she desired. The man brought out a fine tray of rings, earrings and a necklace all encrusted with diamonds. She ran her hands over them and looked at each so carefully and longingly. And then the shop doorbell rang and as the man went to answer it to let another customer in, she grabbed her chance. Pulling all she could from the tray, she rushed past the two men at the door into the street. She was chased by the shopkeeper and the police who were called when the alarm on the tray was triggered. She was caught within a few streets of the shop by an officer and the crowd of shoppers, and was then presented before a judge.

"Why on earth did you think you could get away with the robbery given the number of CCTV cameras, the alarm system and so many people around in the middle of the day?" the judge asked her.

"When I saw the diamonds, I didn't see the risks of stealing them. All I could see was the gems," she replied.

Thus, do we all lose sight of what is really important and matters when we fill our life with desire and greed?

21 ROAST SAUSAGES

A renowned and devout holy woman was travelling one day with a band of her followers. The band of twenty followers had walked all day and had arranged to stay in a barn next to a small cottage at the edge of a village. The family felt greatly honoured to have such a visitor and had planned a small feast in celebration and had invited a number of guests to meet the travelling teacher. After freshening up, the holy woman and her followers joined the party and to thank the family for their hospitality she gave an inspiring talk. The hosts and guests had prepared a feast for the travellers and on each table were delicacies and delights to eat and drink. As they began eating, a number of the devout followers looked decidedly uneasy and the holy woman was aware of a lot of chatter in the room and some heated debates. After they had all eaten, the holy woman offered to take questions from the crowded room.

"I thank you for your kindness and would be delighted to answer any questions that you might have," she said.

The crowd looked rather unsettled and it was evident there were issues on people's minds. After a few moments a villager spoke up. "Well, your holiness, we were somewhat surprised, as were some of your followers, that you ate several pieces of sausage," he stated.

"Well, why not? You kindly provided a splendid feast

for us and I know you have little to spare. I was touched by your generosity and kindness," she replied.

"But, your holiness, I thought you were a strict vegan and not only did you eat the vegetables offered but also the sausage, which, I fear, was made from pork," one of her followers added.

"Indeed, it was, and I understand such sausage is a highly prized delicacy in these parts. Who am I to reject your generosity? I pray you all to remember it is not what goes into your mouth that defiles and spoils you, but what comes out of it!"

22 THE CROW

There was once a beautiful plump pigeon that built a nest close to the chimney of the house – just above the kitchen where the brickwork was warm and dry. The cooks liked her a great deal and enjoyed hearing her coo loudly. They put leftover bread, grains and food scraps outside the kitchen and in exchange she 'sang' for them. She was content and happy, as were the workers.

One afternoon a crow noticed the pigeon and saw how plump and healthy she looked. The crow struck up a friendship with the pigeon and told the bird that in exchange for allowing it to roost by her nest, the crow would protect the pigeon and any youngsters she had from the hawk that lived in a nearby tree. The crow offered good company and kept the hawk away, and the pigeon was happy with the arrangement. The crow, however, had seen how well fed the pigeon was and in part his friendship was designed on cashing in on the food source. On the pretext of just his nosey nature, the crow asked where the food scraps all came from, emphasising he only ate meat and didn't care for grains and the like. The pigeon explained where she got food from and the crow saw the food placed outside the window of the kitchen and he decided that where there was grain, there would be meat.

The pigeon said the crow might like to sing for the

kitchen staff or in some way offer them entertainment to perhaps encourage them to add a few meat scraps. But the crow was greedy and impatient and decided he would visit the kitchen directly for the food. The pigeon cautioned against this, saying the staff wouldn't want a bird flapping about over their food.

One day the crow smelled fish being fried in a pan and his greed got the better of him. He set off to get into the kitchen via the back chimney that wasn't alight. He fluttered down, following the smell and was soon in the kitchen. However, as he flew out of the small back fireplace, his wings caught a ladle which clattered on the stone wall. The cook heard the noise and turned around to see the sooty crow fluttering round in her kitchen. She threw a large tea towel over the crow and caught it. The head gardener took the crow away to a faraway field, maybe to 'help make a pie'! – we shall never know – but what the pigeon knew was that the crow was undone by greed. So, take care when greed comes calling… the price you will pay for your greed is likely to be a heavy one!

23 THE BLACK STALLION

The king decided he needed a new horse, so he called the head of the stables to come before him. The man was told to spare no cost and bring to him the best horse in the land. The man thought for a moment and then declared that he had an old friend who was by far the greatest expert in horses there was and that he would send at once for his best animal. A message soon arrived from the old friend in the country announcing that he would soon be sending a horse as a gift to the king. The whole palace and court were abuzz with excitement and soon the story was that the finest black stallion in the land would be the king's pride… the finest horse in the land.

A few days later, a boy arrived with the horse for the king, but both king and head of stables were surprised to see a brown mare.

"You said your friend was an expert. The greatest expert there was!" the king complained. "Look what he has sent… I was expecting a splendid black stallion. The fact that the horse is brown is bad enough, but it's a mare! Your expert seems to be much less than I had hoped for. He knows little of colour or, for that matter, sex."

It was well known to everyone that stallions were stronger and faster and that a pure black horse would stand out for all to see.

"Ah, my friend assures me this is the finest horse and

that it is better than any other he has seen," the head of stables declared in admiration. "So keen is his sight that he no longer even sees the outer characteristics of the horse, only its inner quality. He knows horses better than any other."

The king remained unconvinced, but was surprised when the horse approached him. It stood perfectly still whilst he mounted it. Indeed, the horse bowed to make it easier for the king to climb onto its back. Once settled, the horse took off, offering such a smooth ride the king had no need for a saddle or indeed reins, and, as for speed, the king was thrilled. He had never ridden such a splendid beast before. He could feel the power of the horse's muscles beneath him and was delighted as the horse leapt over fences and streams without causing him to feel unbalanced. This truly was the best horse he had ever ridden and the king had no doubt it was the finest in the land.

How often do we simply make judgements on exterior and somewhat superficial outer appearances, failing to see the deeper inner qualities?

24 BAD HABITS

A man was so concerned about his son, that he requested that a wise woman help him wean the young man away from his bad habits.

"The boy bites his nails, spends hours on a trivial computer game, eats only unhealthy junk food and has taken up smoking… next it will be drugs and alcohol!" the man wailed.

The wise woman invited the young man to walk with her through her garden. After a few metres, she stopped and asked the son to pull out a small seedling from the ground. The youth held the plant between his thumb and forefinger then pulled it out. They walked on a bit and the woman asked him to pull out a slightly bigger plant. The youth pulled hard and the plant came out, roots and all. Next, she asked him to dislodge a bush from the ground. The youth used all his strength and eventually proudly pulled the whole plant free from the soil.

"What's this all about?" he asked the woman.

She replied with, "Now take this one out," pointing to a small tree.

The youth grasped the trunk and tried to pull it out but it would not move. "That's impossible," said the boy, wiping his brow and breathing deeply with the effort.

"So it is with habits," said the woman. "When they are young, they are quite easy to stop but once they take hold and have become established, they can be very stubborn. Better, of course, not to take up habits in the first place, or try and stop them early. Once they are well established, the challenge will be much greater."

25 THE BLUE SPOT

One day, the teacher entered her classroom and asked her students to prepare for a surprise test. They all waited anxiously at their desks for the exam to begin. She handed out the exam sheets with the text facing down, as usual. Once she had handed them all out, she asked the students to turn over the papers. To everyone's surprise, there were no questions on the sheet, just a blue spot in the centre of the paper. The teacher noticed the looks of surprise and told the students the following, "All you have to do is write about what you see on the paper." The students, although puzzled by this, got started.

At the end of the class, the teacher took all the papers in and started reading each one of them out loud in front of all the students. Every student had described the blue spot and explored its position in the centre of the sheet, its size and the exact colour of blue that it was. After all the answers had been read, the classroom fell silent and the teacher explained.

"I'm not going to grade you on this test, I just wanted to give you something to think about. No one wrote about the white part of the paper. Everyone focused on the blue spot. The same thing happens in our lives. We all focus on the blue spots... the health issues that bother us, the lack of money, the complicated relationship with a family member, the disappointment with a friend, the mistakes we make. The dark spots in our life are often very small when compared to everything we have and do in our lives, but we still focus on them. Take your minds away from the blue spots and look at the white… the blessings in your life, and be happy and contented. It might also be helpful if we were to treat others by reflecting on the white aspects of goodness rather than focusing on the 'blue spot' shortcomings!

26 PEACE OF MIND

Once a wise teacher was walking from one town to another town with a few of his followers. As they walked, they passed a lake. They stopped to rest in the shade of some trees and the teacher remarked to one of his disciples that he was thirsty so asked him to get some water from the lake. The disciple walked up to the water's edge. When he reached it, he noticed that some people were washing clothes in the water and, right at that moment, a bullock cart started crossing through the lake. As a result, the water became very muddy. The disciple thought the water would be unfit to drink and taste poor, so he returned to the teacher and told him this information.

Half an hour later, the teacher asked the same disciple to go back to the lake and get him some water to drink. The disciple obediently went back to the lake and this time he found that the lake had absolutely clear water in it. The mud had settled down and the water above it looked fit to be drunk. So, he collected some water in a pot and brought it to the teacher. The teacher looked at the water, and then he looked up at the disciple and said, "See what you did to make the water clean… you let it be. The mud settled down on its own to give you clear water. Your mind is also like that. When it is disturbed, just let it be. Give it time and it will settle down on its own. You don't have to put in any effort to calm it down. It will happen. It is effortless. Just let go!"

Having 'peace of mind' is not a strenuous job, it is an effortless process. When there is peace inside you, that peace permeates to the outside. It spreads around you and in the environment, such that people around start feeling that peace and grace. So, the next time your head fills with worries, concerns and agitation, let go and over time the clouds in your mind will settle and your mind will clear on its own. And do remember – what you resist, persists. Wrestling with a troubled mind – will keep it troubled!

27 THE LAWN

A man who took great pride in his lawn found himself with a large crop of dandelions and assorted weeds amongst the grass. Each week he raked the lawn and carefully mowed it, and twice a year he applied lawn feed. Yet the grass was always overwhelmed by weeds and the lawn always looked poor. He read books, rang a radio station phone-in and spent hours on the internet looking for solutions. He tried everything, including writing to the Department of Agriculture. He listed all the things he had tried over the years and closed his letter with the question: "What shall I do now?"

In due course, the reply came, listing all the things he had already tried.

One afternoon he was walking in the countryside, along a cliff path, when he came across an elderly man sitting on a bench overlooking the sea. After talking for a while, he discovered the elderly man was a gardener and lover of wildlife. He seized the opportunity and asked the man about his lawn. The old man suggested doing nothing, not even cutting the grass for a whole year and offered to call the man in a year's time to see how he had got on.

The following year the elderly man called and was greeted with an outpouring of thanks.

"Well, last year the lawn cost me nothing, no expensive treatments and not even any time spent cutting, and the area is covered in amazing flowers and plants, and the garden is full of insects and birds. What I was seeking was perfection and that of course never happens. I had wanted my lawn to be free of imperfections, forgetting we all have imperfections and need to learn to accept them."

Striving to be perfect is both expensive and destined to fail, as does seeking that bowling green lawn. The man now had a meadow full of so many different plants and indeed other wildlife. So, in our lives, start accepting the imperfections and realise nothing is ever perfect.

28 BREAD AND CHEESE

There was once a poor man who ate a simple diet and liked nothing more than bread and cheese. Indeed, most days he only ate plain food that cost him little, such as baked potatoes, simple soups and inexpensive stews. His neighbour called upon him one day and was invited to stay and eat lunch with him.

"Is that all we are having? Bread, soup and fruit?" the neighbour asked, clearly disappointed at the simple food. "At my home we always have five courses, with several roast meats and plenty of freshly cooked vegetable and delicious seasonal fruits. And we often leave the table with plenty of food left over. Now, if you came and worked twelve-hour night shifts at the factory I work in six days a week, you would need to eat a much better diet to ensure you were not left feeling hungry."

"Ah yes," replied the poor man, "but if you learned to eat a simple diet like I do, you wouldn't need to work all night, six nights a week and have no time to enjoy the world and your life."

The story reminded me of the holiday maker in his private yacht who moored it at a small jetty next to a local fisherman in a battered old boat in which he had caught a few fish to feed his family. The man in the yacht suggested to the local fisherman that if he worked harder and longer hours, he could catch more fish and could sell the excess and soon would have money to buy a bigger boat. He could then fish further out and catch even more and get even more money. He could then buy a much bigger boat, catch even more, sell more and buy an even bigger boat that would allow him to be away overnight, filling the boat with fish and making lots of money. He could then buy two boats and employ men to fish for him and go on a holiday.

"Yes, but where might I go on holiday?" the fisherman asked.

"You could come here in a motor yacht like me and sit and watch the sun go down."

"I do that every day," said the fisherman. "You only manage two weeks a year. I think I'll stay where I am!"

29 THE COFFIN

There was once a farmer who worked hard all his life and built up a very successful business. He built a splendid farmhouse and with his wife raised three sons, who gave them several grandchildren. His eldest son lived with his own family on the farm after the farmer's wife died and as the farmer got older he handed over more of the business to his son. The time soon came when the elderly farmer spent his days sitting in a rocking chair on the porch or playing with his grandchildren. He was no longer strong enough to work.

Resentment soon arose in the son's mind and he began to look on his father as a drain and just another mouth to feed. The son was preoccupied with having to work so hard that he forgot his father had worked to build up the farm and began to think of him as that useless old man on the porch. Eventually, he began to think the old man didn't need to be around anymore, so he built a big box of heavy teak. As soon as it was finished, he wheeled it in his barrow to the porch and told the old man to climb inside. The old man did as he was asked and as soon as he was inside, the son closed the lid and locked the clasp. The son wheeled to barrow to the nearby cliffs and was about to tip the box over into the sea to rid himself of the parasitic old man when from inside he heard knocking.

"What do you want?" said the son gruffly.

From inside he heard his father speak. "I understand you want to get rid of me and that you think I am now a burden upon you and your family. But think carefully. If you want to be rid of me, take me out of the box and just throw me over the cliff into the sea. That way you will save the box. After all, your children might have need of it in a few years' time!"

30 THE LOST HORSE

A horse breeder in North America lost his best stallion one day, when it jumped the fence of the corral at his ranch and ran off into the countryside. He searched for it for two weeks and finally decided it was probably gone forever. He told his neighbour who said he would look out for it and expressed his regrets. The breeder merely replied, "Who knows what is good and what is bad."

The very next day, the stallion returned, bringing with him three wild mares. The neighbour rushed over to celebrate with the breeder, but the old farmer simply said, "Who knows what is good and what is bad."

The following day, the breeder's son fell from one of the wild mares while trying to break her in and broke his arm and injured his leg. The neighbour came by to check on the son and see if he could help, but the old breeder just said, "Who knows what is good and what is bad."

The next day the army came to the farm to conscript the farmer's son for the war. The recruiting sergeant found the son an invalid who was still unable to walk unaided, let alone fight and therefore left him with his father. The neighbour thought to himself, "Who knows what is good and what is bad."

I wonder how true this is in our lives. One spring I met a homeless chap that I had often seen in my town, but who I feared had died in the cold winter we had endured.

I offered to buy him a hot drink and a sandwich – but he refused telling me after eight years on the streets he had got a room and was cooking and caring for himself. He looked well and for the first time was smartly dressed and looked well fed.

He told me that the previous autumn he had hit rock bottom and was arrested for being drunk and disorderly for about the twentieth time and had got a prison sentence. At the time, he said it was devastating being locked up, but in six months he had not been able to get any alcohol, had slept in a bed, got regular meals and showered every day. He'd had a television to watch and had got a job as a wing cleaner. A charity then hooked up with him and helped him find a room and job when he left prison… who knows what is good or bad!

31 THE DISHONEST STUDENT

There was once a famous teacher and people came from far and wide to study and stay with him. He had many followers and students who lived at his home, slept in dormitories in the grounds and each day would have lessons on life, philosophy and righteous living. Unfortunately, one of the students was not too honest and, amongst other 'crimes', used to steal food, bed linen and books. His fellow students found out, and told the teacher and they asked that the student should be thrown out or punished. The teacher did nothing and later when the student was caught in a similar act, his colleagues again complained to the teacher. Once more, the teacher did nothing.

After several weeks of a number of small items going missing, the students got together and confronted the teacher, telling him that he should punish the student and if he did not, they would all leave and his work would come to an end.

The teacher listened to their request and asked to meet all the students that evening. He told them that most of them were wise and should be pleased that amongst all their lessons they had learnt the importance of honesty and that they clearly knew right from wrong. And such was their wisdom that they were free to leave his studies as they had much to offer the wider world. Indeed, they could leave and teach others, as well as learn elsewhere. He then announced that the one amongst them who had taken things was not free to leave. "He doesn't even know right from wrong, and who will teach him if I do not? I will allow him to stay here even if all the rest of you leave."

Tears flooded the face of the dishonest student, for all desire to steal had vanished, such was his learning from this day.

32 THE TEAPOT

Zyphir was a young man who lived in a big city with his parents and who each holiday, would go and stay in the nearby countryside with his grandparents. His grandmother was a gentle woman who had a prize possession: a large china teapot that had been passed down through her family and which stood on the dresser in the front room of her cottage. Zyphir had never seen the teapot used. It was too valuable to his grandmother to risk it getting broken, so there it remained in pride of place on the dresser.

One afternoon whilst staying at the cottage, Zyphir was playing with a kitten. He was pulling a ball of fluff along the ground on a string for the kitten to chase. The kitten would lunge and pounce on the ball of fluff and Zyphir would squeal with delight. As he ran backwards tugging the fluff behind him, he entered the front room and smacked right into the dresser. He watched with horror as the teapot toppled off the dresser and hit the ground, breaking into many pieces. Zyphir quickly picked the pieces up and placed them in a bag. Just as he had picked up the last piece his grandmother came into the room. Zyphir held the bag behind him and quickly asked her, "Why do people have to die?"

Grandmother thought for a few moments and replied,

"It's natural, it's the way it is. Everything dies eventually and everything has just so long to live."

At this, Zyphir held forward the bag with the broken teapot. "It was time for your teapot to die."

We will all experience the loss of loved ones, made worse in part because we fail to accept that nothing lasts or lives forever. This alone gives us good reason to make the most of our time and to appreciate what we have whilst we have it.

33 THE FROG AND THE GOLDFISH

The warty frog, who was a dull shade of green with streaks of grey, sat at the side of the pond enjoying the warmth of the sun. In the pond lived a prize goldfish who spotted the frog and swam over to where he sat under a large leaf.

"Greetings, my frog friend," said the goldfish.

The frog blinked in reply, at which the goldfish said, "Don't you see how beautiful I have become?"

Again, the frog blinked. The goldfish jumped out of the water and landed close to where the frog sat.

"Can you see the sun glisten and sparkle off my golden scales?" said the goldfish.

The frog blinked once more but made no reply.

"I can't understand your silence," said the goldfish. "I have such grace and beauty, and you do nothing but sit and blink."

Again, the frog merely blinked and sat still. The fish came to the surface of the pond and rolled over, displaying its blue and silver underside that sparkled like so many diamonds in the sky.

"Come on, old frog, say something… you cannot fail to be dazzled by my shiny scales. Am I not the best goldfish you have ever seen?"

The frog blinked once more.

"Come on, old frog, you must agree there is no other

goldfish that has my beauty, stunning coloured skin and sleek fins."

The frog blinked once more and as it did, a waiting crane speared the sparkling fish and flew off into the sky.

"Bye bye," croaked the frog.

Maybe we would do better to be more like the frog… say less and adopt a lower profile, for, as they say, put your head above the crowd and someone will take a swipe at it.

34 THE WATER BEARER

A water bearer in India had two large pots that hung on either end of a pole which he carried across his shoulders and neck. One of the pots had a crack in it, while the other pot was perfect. It was a long walk from the well to the house and on each trip the cracked pot arrived only half full. Every day for a full two years, the bearer delivered only one and a half pots full of water to his master's house. Of course, the perfect pot was proud of its accomplishments, it was as perfect as the day it was made. The cracked pot was ashamed of its imperfection and sad that it was able to accomplish only half of what it had been made to do.

After two years of what it perceived to be a bitter failure, it spoke to the water bearer one day by the stream. "I am ashamed of myself, and I want to apologise to you."

"Why?" asked the bearer. "What are you ashamed of?"

"I have been able, for these past two years, to deliver only half my load because this crack in my side causes water to leak out all the way back to your master's house. Because of this flaw, you have to do all of this work, and you don't get full value from your efforts," the pot said.

The water bearer's heart went out to the old cracked pot, and, in his compassion, he said, "As we return to the master's house, I want you to notice the beautiful flowers along the path."

Indeed, as they went up the hill, the old cracked pot took notice of the sun warming the beautiful wild flowers on the side of the path, and this cheered it some. But at the end of the trail, it still felt sad because it had leaked out half its load, and so again it apologised to the bearer for its failure.

The bearer said to the pot, "Did you notice that there were flowers only on your side of the path, but not on the other pot's side? That's because I have always known about your flaw, and I took advantage of it. I planted flower seeds on your side of the path and every day while we walk back from the stream, you have watered them. For two years I have been able to pick these beautiful flowers to decorate my master's table. Without you being just the way you are, he would not have this beauty to grace his house."

It is not only from our good deeds that good things arise. Sometimes our limitations bring forth the greatest glory.

35 THE TRAVELLER

There was once a traveller who went from place to place seeking wisdom and understanding. He never settled for long in any one town, preferring to keep moving to seek out new experiences and acquaintances from who he might learn. He took shelter where he could, often sleeping in caves, hedgerows and derelict out buildings or accepting hospitality in exchange for work. He did odd jobs such as cleaning and labouring to earn enough money for food, and he made few demands upon the world.

One afternoon he came across a shepherd on the hillside tending his flock of sheep. He greeted the shepherd with a friendly smile and wished him a good day. The shepherd invited him to share the stew he was making over an open fire, and the two men were soon exchanging tales of their lives and fortunes. Thinking of where he might stay that night, the traveller asked the shepherd, "What kind of weather are we going to have today?"

The shepherd replied, "The kind of weather I like."

This answer puzzled the traveller who replied, "How do you know it will be the kind of weather you like?"

The shepherd replied, "Having found out, sir, that I cannot always get what I like, I have learned to always like what I get. So, I am quite sure we will have the kind of weather I like."

36 TWO RABBITS

A martial arts student was desperate to learn more and improve his skills so asked all his fellow pupils who he should go to for help. He went to all the teachers that were recommended and made some progress but was impatient to be the best. He eventually left home to travel to the big city to seek out the most famous teachers in all the land.

After travelling several days, he arrived at a famous teacher's house and knocked on the door. He was surprised to see the teacher was a slight man who was clearly older than his own grandfather and he feared he would learn little from him, but arranged to return the next day. Fearing he might not learn enough with this teacher, he went to another famous teacher living in the city and arranged to be taught by him as well. He would surely become the very best as he had arranged to be taught by the two best teachers in the city.

The following day he went to the first teacher to start his lessons. "I want to be the very best in the land at martial arts. So, in addition to learning from you in the morning, I will study in the afternoon with master Wei who lives nearby and who uses a different style," he proudly announced.

The old man thought for a while and then said, "Imagine the wily fox... he has sat for twenty minutes waiting for a rabbit to show from underground. His luck suddenly changes as not one but two rabbits pop up from their burrows at once. After waiting to be sure they have settled to eat, he sets off in chase, sure he will eat well that night. As he gets closer, he is not sure which will be easiest to catch – first the one on the right, then the one on the left, or maybe the right. In the confusion in his mind, he is soon thwarted as both rabbits pop back underground. The hunter who chases two rabbits," answered the master, "catches neither one."

Maybe we are like that hunter and need to concentrate on one thing at a time, too often not doing so well because, like the student, we are hunting two rabbits at once!

37 THE MIGHTY EMPEROR

There was once a mighty emperor who was known for his foul temper. One evening he entered the bedroom of his soon-to-be-bride, the most beautiful woman in all the land. She was being made to marry him against her will by her parents who owed the emperor a great debt.

The woman sat in the room, expressionless, staring at the wall.

"Hello, my beautiful wife-to-be," he said, but she did not reply. "I said hello to you and you will respond when I address you, do you understand me? For I am the emperor and will be obeyed," he snarled.

But still, she didn't reply. He was not used to being ignored and despite his anger at her failure to respond, he was curious, and gruffly asked, "What on earth are you thinking, sitting there ignoring me?"

Finally, she answered him. "Two things. One, I do not wish to marry you because you are so rude and demanding. And two, I was wondering if you really have so much power that you could change anything you want."

"What?" the emperor exclaimed with outrage. "How dare you question my authority and my right to demand anything I want! I have it within my power to snap my fingers and whatever I command within my kingdom will be obeyed."

"There is no doubting the power you have, but I truly

wonder if you have the power to change everything and anything."

"What is it you are wondering if I could change?" roared the emperor, who by now was growing very impatient.

"Your attitude," she replied. And with that she got up and walked out of the room, leaving him in stunned silence.

We may feel we are all powerful and indeed may have thrown our weight around, but are we up to the biggest challenge of all… to change our attitudes?

38 THE RAT AND THE CAT

There once lived a farmer who was plagued by a large and clever rat who had the run of the farmhouse. This annoyed the farmer no end so he went to the village to buy a cat. A street trader sold him a splendid black cat that he said would catch the rat. Indeed, the cat was very lean and fit looking. But the rat was even quicker than the cat and after a week with no success, the farmer returned the cat.

This time the trader offered him a large and grizzled cat and guaranteed that no rat could escape this master mouser. The rat knew enough to stay clear of this tough alley cat, but when the cat slept, the rat ran about. Half the day the rat would hide, but the other half he again had run of the farmhouse. The farmer brought this cat back to the vender who shook his head in despair saying he had given the farmer his best cats and there was nothing more he could do.

Returning home with his money, the farmer met a neighbour and asked his advice. After hearing the famer's story, the neighbour offered him the services of the cat that lived in his home. The cat was old and fat and he scarcely seemed to notice when he was carried away by the doubtful farmer.

For two weeks the cat did little more than sleep all day and night. The farmer wanted to give the cat back to the neighbour as it was eating so much and achieving nothing. The neighbour insisted he keep him a while longer, assuring him the rat's days were close to an end.

The rat became accustomed to the presence of the lazy old cat and was soon up to his old tricks even, on occasion, brazenly dancing around the old cat as he slept. Then one day, as the rat went about his business without any concern, he passed close by the cat who swiftly struck out his paw and pinned the rat to the floor, dispatching him.

Sometimes we do better to sit patiently waiting for the right opportunity to come by!

39 THE BANDIT AND THE TEACHER

A wise teacher was sitting one afternoon in her garden, offering thoughts and pearls of wisdom to a group of followers. She had become extremely popular and as a result a number of other teachers had become jealous of her and decided to send round a local bandit to disrupt her meeting and attack her. The bandit had been paid well to terrorise the teacher's followers and was intent on using a heavy hammer to smash up the out-house where the teacher was sitting.

The teacher saw the bandit approach and, before he could strike a blow, addressed him. "I see you come with thoughts of doing harm and causing havoc," the teacher said. "Might I suggest you first show us your strength and power by cutting a large branch from that tree, to fill our hearts with fear and dread."

The bandit liked this idea… to make everyone notice his immense power and display his strength.

"One slash and I am sure you could take off the biggest branch," the teacher continued.

The bandit was keen to show his might and, with a single blow, he lopped off the biggest branch. It fell crashing to the ground, sending fear through the hearts of all the followers.

"What now?" screamed the bandit.

"Put it back," said the teacher.

The bandit laughed. "You must be crazy to think that anyone can do that."

"Oh no, it is you who are crazy to think that you are mighty because you can wound and destroy. That is a task that anyone can do. Those that are really powerful are the ones that can create and heal."

Are we amongst those that feel we show our power by acts of aggression or violence, or do we show real power by bringing about healing and creativity?

40 OYSTERS

There were once two beautiful plump oysters that sat together on the seabed. They had found a spot where the water in the ocean was warm and the gentle current brought a rich supply of food particles for them to filter out.

One afternoon a speed boat went past the site and stirred up the grit and sand on the seabed, covering them with debris. Both oysters were pleased at this at first as the material that washed over them brought a bountiful harvest of material that they could eat. However, after a couple of days, one of the oysters expressed concern that as well as taking in food stuff, it had taken in a piece of grit that had got stuck in its soft flesh. The second oyster agreed that this was annoying as indeed it had also taken on board a piece of sharp grit. The first oyster became very irritated by the piece of grit and complained constantly that the speed boat had ruined its life. The second oyster grew fed up with this constant moaning and decided to move from its rich spot to elsewhere in the ocean where the chance of being covered in grit would be less.

The second oyster found itself in a bed with several other oysters and told them why it had moved. It stayed in this spot for many years and lived a happy and contented life until one afternoon its old neighbour moved into the bed. The second oyster was surprised and disappointed that the first oyster continued to moan about the boat incident that had occurred all that time ago. The first oyster was intrigued that its old neighbour seemed to have moved on and had forgotten the day their lives were so disrupted. Eventually, it asked for an explanation.

"Well, that's easy, you can't always choose what happens to you but you can choose what you do about it. I see you have chosen to moan about it for a lifetime!"

That afternoon the local fishermen were diving near the oyster bed and the two oysters were both caught. Upon opening the first oyster, the fisherman saw the rich meat inside and decided it was one for the pot. On opening the second oyster, the fisherman found the beautiful pearl, the biggest and best he had ever seen. He took the pearl, which would make him very rich, then thanked the oyster and returned it to the ocean in the hopes it might grow another pearl.

You see, without a piece of grit to form the centre, no oyster can grow a pearl. So, remember that whilst you do not always choose what happens to you, you can and do choose what you do about it. Try turning everything that goes against your wishes and interests into an opportunity to learn and grow.

41 THE CHILLIES

One afternoon, a man walked into the local market. Sitting by one stall was a merchant who was selling bright red chillies. Each week, he came to sell his chillies and people would buy them to take home and cut into small pieces to use in cooking... they were too hot to use whole.

One day, the people at the market were surprised to see a man approach the seller and buy a chilli. Instead of taking it home, the man popped it into his mouth and chewed it for a while before swallowing it. His face turned red and his eyes watered and he quickly followed the chilli with a mouthful of yoghurt to cool his mouth. He then bought another chilli and did the same things.

Soon a crowd of people gathered round the stall to watch this remarkable feat. People raised concerns that he would become ill and placed bets on how many chillies he would be able to eat. Even the stall holder bet that he would not manage more than ten.

After each chilli, the man's face became redder and he needed a bigger helping of yoghurt to quell the burning sensation in his mouth and throat. As he reached for his fifteenth chilli, the stall holder asked him, "What, friend, are you doing? You will set your mouth on fire if you continu. Even I had not expected you to pass ten!"

"Simple," said the man. "I'm looking for the sweet one!"

Have we been in a similar situation? Doing the same thing over and over again and expecting different results? This, of course, is the famous definition of insanity. And maybe it is something we suffer from. Remember, if you always do what you've always done, you'll always get the same results. And, if that isn't working, try anything else!

42 THE STALL HOLDERS

A market stall holder turned up early one morning to set up his stall when he noticed another merchant had arrived before him and had taken his 'pitch'. A row broke out and the early arriver, who had taken the pitch, accused the stall holder of being greedy – always taking this spot and not allowing anyone else to set up in the position. The stall holder asserted his right to the spot and it was at the point that the early arriver was threatening violence that the market manager came across. He explained that plots were allocated by the committee and that the early arriver should move to where he had been allocated a place. As he reluctantly moved, the early arriver continued to hurl abuse and make offensive comments about the second stall holder.

A week later, two other stall holders spoke to the second man and said they were surprised at how unpleasant the early arriver had been and said the man should make it clear in no uncertain terms that he would not put up with such threats and unpleasantness. He told them he had written a stern letter to the man, setting out his concerns about the threats made and making it clear he found the encounter very upsetting. The letter went on to say that such threats were totally unacceptable and that a civilised man would never make such an unpleasant scene and that he had upset all the other stall holders by being so nasty.

The two other stall holders asked him how the man had responded to such a fierce letter.

"Oh, I don't know, I didn't send it and I never do. When something like that upsets me, I spend time setting out my thoughts on paper, but I never send them."

This was a strategy that Abraham Lincoln used when someone upset or annoyed him. He realised that reacting and flying off the handle always led to matters getting worse and it is interesting that a number of Lincoln's letters survive him, still unsent in his work papers! How often have you reacted to another person's actions or comments and spoken out or acted in haste? As the old saying goes… act in haste, repent at leisure!

43 THE HORIZON

Two young men sat on a hill one day arguing about how far away the horizon was.

"It's at least five miles to that fir tree on the skyline," said the first.

"I'd say more like eight," said the other.

As they argued, an elderly woman came by and listening to them bickering, she suggested they walked to it. If they took twenty minutes per mile as a rough estimate, they would soon know if the horizon was five or eight miles away.

After six hours, the two young men had not come back and, growing worried that they might have got lost, she asked her daughter to take her in their four-wheel drive vehicle to look for them.

The two ladies soon reached the fir tree, from where, a long way off in the distance they spotted the two young men still walking away.

After another twenty five minutes, they caught up with the men.

"Now where are you going?" she asked.

"Well, we reckoned the tree was about six and a half miles away, but as we got nearer to it, we realised it wasn't on the horizon and we spotted a row of low bushes that were now on the horizon, but that was three miles back. We are now off to that hill ridge which we think is another five miles, and then we will arrive at the horizon."

The elderly lady smiled and turned to the young men and gave these wise words. "Your search for the horizon is like the search many of us make to be fully content in life. It is a goal we can never reach. Had you walked for long enough you would eventually appear from behind your starting point, having walked right round the world!"

And this indeed is like our happiness. We might reach smaller goals on the way, such as a good job, a good wage, a delightful home, an ideal partner and the latest car model, but still the horizon of full contentment is one we can never reach. We should realise that desires are often impossible to fulfil and that yearning for what we don't have stops us from appreciating what we do have!

44 SHARPEN THE SAW

Two skilled woodsmen were at a country fair where they entered a challenge to saw a large tree trunk in half in the fastest time. Each man stood over the log to be cut and in turn each chose a saw from the box offered to them by the judge. The crowd anticipated a close run thing as each man was a champion woodsman in their own right.

At the appointed time, the judge dropped his handkerchief, indicating the men could start. The man on the right quickly rolled up his sleeves, spat on his hands and picked up the saw and started cutting and quickly made inroads into the wood. The second man carefully inspected the blade and carefully took a file and tool and set to sharpening the blade.

There was sawdust everywhere as the first man had cut one third of the way through and was looking very pleased with himself. Eventually the second man was happy with the blade and set to cutting his log. He had made a good start when he noticed his opponent was almost half way through.

As the cutting continued, the second woodman made steady progress and was clearly catching up. However, his opponent was now well into the last third, but his cutting strokes were shorter, his face red and sweat was pouring off his torso. The second woodsman looked very composed and was making full and effective strokes through the wood. The crowd were roaring the two men on and those that had placed wagers on the first man were looking set to claim their winnings. But the second man was cutting as well now as at the start and had soon cut through the log. He turned to see how his opponent was getting on, only to see him collapsed on the ground with still a fair bit to cut.

Which woodsman are you? Rush in and get on with things or take time to carefully prepare? Often, we do better by taking time to be fully prepared.

45 THE VICAR AND THE POLICEMAN

You have been out for the evening and catch the last train home. You take a seat opposite two people in the middle of the carriage where it will be less draughty and quieter. It's never a busy service and you notice that opposite you sits a woman who is smartly dressed with a navy-blue shirt and a vicar's dog collar. She makes good eye contact and had smiled at you when you came and sat down. Next to her is a man in a police officers' uniform; he has short cropped hair, a couple of day's beard growth and doesn't make any eye contact.

As the journey progresses, you notice the policeman looks almost constantly out of the window and has the same fixed expression on his face. The vicar appears relaxed and animated and, if you catch her eye, she politely smiles and carries on reading her book. After about forty minutes you decide you need to go to the toilet. You look up and notice a sign on the carriage wall indicating the direction of the toilet. As you stand up, you realise the carriage is almost empty, except for a few passengers sitting near both exits. The policeman looks at you and makes you feel uncomfortable so you feel obliged to speak. "I'm just nipping to the loo. Keep an eye on my seat if you would." You realise it sounds a bit stupid, given the carriage is almost empty, but he makes eye contact and nods at you.

As you leave the carriage to go to the toilet, you are pulled roughly to one side by two men. "Stay still and be quiet. Thank goodness you've left the carriage. There's a dangerous man on board, who's armed and we are planning to take him down!" You realise the few people you did pass did not acknowledge you and the two men tell you slowly the carriage has been filled with undercover officers at each end.

"He's wearing a police uniform and looks very suspicious. He made me feel uncomfortable," you blurt out as you tell them you are bursting to use the toilet.

After using the toilet, you come out to find there are four men standing in the area outside the carriage door; two of them have sub-machine guns!

"Right, that way," they say and push you towards the next carriage along.

As you enter the carriage, two uniformed police officers approach you and take you to a table area and sit you opposite to them. They tell you of the dangerous criminal that is on the train and that they suspect he is armed.

"And, dressed as a policeman," you add!

"This service," crackles a voice over the train public address, "is running behind a slow train and we are to be held briefly at the next station. This is not a scheduled stop and the doors will not be open – do not attempt to leave the train."

Within minutes the train lurches to a halt and the two officers march you to the doorway and put you off the train together with several other passengers. You are made to move along the platform away from the carriage you had been sitting in originally and the train pulls away. You are taken to a waiting room and thanked for cooperating and are taken home by police car. You are told nothing else.

The following morning, you hear on the radio that the fugitive has been arrested and no one was hurt and you tell your partner how you had got caught up in it all.

"I reckon he had taken that poor vicar hostage and was trying to escape dressed as a police officer," you tell your partner.

"Oh no," she says, "the fugitive was the man dressed as a female vicar. The police officer sat next to him was travelling home by train as his car had broken down and was unaware that it was him, so good was this disguise."

How often are we taken in by appearances? Don't judge by looks, sight or sound… judge by character and behaviour.

46 THE X-RAY!

I went last week for an X-ray on my foot after I dropped the iron on it and found I couldn't easily walk two days later! The doctor sent me to X-ray and when I arrived in the waiting room there were several other people there. I took a numbered card and took a seat to wait my turn. After a few minutes, the man next to me turned and said, "This makes me so mad – I've been sitting here thirty minutes and no one seems to be moving!"

I sat quietly reading a magazine, appreciative of not having to tidy the garage, mow the lawn or wash the car. A couple of people went in and had X-rays and still only number 14 was showing – I was number 19.

"Oh, my word, still three people to go. I am beginning to get really annoyed," the chap next to me blurted out.

I nodded politely in his direction and got on with my magazine and thought about the rubbish at the back of the garage that I ought to move. I noticed it had started raining and realised that this would mean the mower would stay idle and the back of the garage could wait and all the dust would wash off in the rain and I might finish this interesting article!

"Oh, now look at that, it's raining and there are still three people in front of me – I'm going to lose it soon," my neighbour ranted. "These waiting rooms make me so angry. Don't you get wound up just sitting here?"

Risking a black eye, I replied, "I am enjoying sitting here reading and not having to do anything for an hour or so. I get little time to just sit. Mind you, I am beginning to feel a bit irritated."

"I'm not surprised, we've been here hours and no one seems to be moving," he butted in.

"Well, what I find slightly irritating," I said, "is you going on about being angry and irritated!"

No one and nothing can make you angry. Like my 'friend', you can choose to be angry about almost anything… but only if you choose to. He not only chose to be annoyed by the wait, he was not best pleased by the rain. Not that it would worry the rain that he was grumpy, or that by being annoyed could he stop the rain!

47 THE WORRY TREE

One day I hired a carpenter to help me on a house renovation project that I was undertaking. We had worked hard all day on the old farmhouse and I had been impressed with his workmanship. He had got a puncture in his van that made him late arriving, his electric saw stopped working during the afternoon and he had to saw the timber by hand and now his old van refused to start. As he lived on my route home, I gave him a life and he sat in stony silence as if all the cares of the world were on his shoulders. On arriving at his house, he invited me in to meet his family. As we walked toward the front door, he stopped briefly at a small tree in his front garden and stroked the tips of the branches with both hands. After he opened the front door, he underwent an amazing transformation. His face lit up and a big smile spread over it and he hugged his two small children and gave his wife a kiss.

Afterward he walked with me back to my car and I offered to pick him up the following morning. As we passed the tree, my curiosity got the better of me and I asked him about what I had seen him do earlier.

"Ah, that's my worry tree," he replied. "I know I can't help having difficulties and challenges during the day at work, but I am sure of one thing, troubles don't belong in the house with my wife and children. So, I just hang my worries up in the tree every night when I come home. Then in the morning I go and pick them up again."

"Funny thing is," he smiled, "when I come out in the morning to pick them up, there aren't nearly as many there as I remember hanging up the night before."

We don't actually need a real tree but we can all imagine hanging our worries up at night and will be delighted in the morning that many of them are no longer there.

48 THE SPLENDID MEAL

Two students of a famous spiritual teacher decided to spend a week at the master's retreat. The days were to be filled with work, teaching, contemplation and study of ancient texts. One meal was served each day at midday and it consisted of rice and a few vegetables and lentils and for the rest of the day, the students were only permitted water to drink.

By the fourth day, the two students were tiring of the meal and spoke to the master telling him they wanted a change in the food provided. The master agreed to make changes and at lunch time the two students went to the kitchen for their meal at midday and found the cook was not there and no food was set out. The master was sitting at the kitchen table so they asked him what was for lunch.

"I have made changes as you requested – today the meal will be at nine o'clock this evening."

The two students were dismayed and went off to their studies and work feeling rather disappointed as they knew to question the master would be pointless.

As the day progressed, they grew more and more hungry and at nine o'clock when the meal was served, they both thanked the cook and said how good the food was. The master than spoke to them and pointed out it was the same food that they had eaten for the previous three days so why was it that today they were so grateful and complimentary to the cook. The men were not sure and had to agree the food they had moaned about that morning did indeed taste so much better today. The master told them that it was because today they were really hungry and all too often when people sit to eat, they do so out of habit and not because they feel hungry.

My mother used to say to myself and my sister that we would eat the food in front of us if we were really hungry… even if it was sprouts or cauliflower which neither of us liked.

Next time you complain about the food you are given, – don't eat it and once you have missed a few meals, it is surprising what will taste good when you are really hungry. We should of course appreciate that we have food to eat. Imagine living in England a hundred and fifty years ago when most workers had two loaves of bread and some thick soup to eat most days, if not every day.

49 THE MAN AND THE TIGER

One day, a man decided to explore the forest that surrounded his village. He was advised by the head person of the village to take great care as many wild animals lived there and he might be placing himself in danger, but that he was sure to see many wonderful things.

As he entered the forest, the man decided to put a nick into the tree bark of each large tree he passed so that he might find his way back if any danger arose. He was soon delighted to see many beautiful creatures and plants. Hanging from the trees were vines covered in splendid flowers of all colours and giving off a powerful fragrance that filled the air with perfume. There were birds of all colours and sizes that he caught a glimpse of as they flew between the dense trees. And at each small opening he found that, if he approached with care and trod quietly, he saw deer and small mammals as well as snakes, insects and lizards.

He was enthralled by the beauty of the forest and was so absorbed by the sights, sounds and smells that he missed the large hungry tiger that was following him. Twice he sensed he was being followed and turned quickly to see what was behind him, but as he turned there was nothing. Finally, he decided to hide behind a large tree and spring out to see what was following him. As he jumped out, he saw on the path, thirty metres away, a large and very hungry-looking tiger stalking towards him. As he looked at the creature, it raced towards him. He stood frozen to the spot and was about to be devoured when, from a large branch above his head, a burly fellow reached down and grabbed him. The tiger's leap ended with it crashing into the undergrowth.

The man turned to his rescuer, thanked him and asked why had the tiger chosen him to try and eat when there was so much prey in the forest. The fellow that had pulled him to safety turned to him and said, "Maybe it was your fault for being so appetising?"

I wonder to what extent we become a victim of our own conduct and behaviour. If we go around putting ourselves down, being downcast, pessimistic and grumpy – why be surprised that we are attacked or put upon by others? Had the man crept quietly through the forest like the other prey animals, he would not have attracted the tiger's attention.

50 THE MAN AND HIS DOG

A nomadic tribesman decided one day to seek out the famed oasis in the desert near to his encampment, accompanied by his faithful dog. He had heard there were bandits in the desert that would rob him and wild dogs that might attack him, but these would be put off by his own dog.

He set off knowing it would take several days of walking and sleeping in the dunes under the stars, but he knew the riches to be had at the oasis would make it worthwhile. The oasis had date trees with the very best dates, as well as grapes and figs fit for a king, and it was famed for its crystal clear water at the centre of the lush growth, that was the finest anyone had ever tasted.

He walked in the early morning and in the evening – sleeping by night and during the heat of the day. He saw few other travellers and when he did, he stopped to extend his goodwill and to check he was on the right route. He had walked from late afternoon until it was almost dark and today had seen no one. He feared he had lost his way and thought he was at least ten hours walk from the oasis. He fell to the ground exhausted, and knew he should not walk on in the dark.

He set up his camp and felt so miserable that he began weeping into his hands, fearing he had brought disaster onto himself and his trusty dog. They would surely perish in the desert if he could not find the way. Out of the darkness he heard a sound and feared he was to be set upon by bandits and would die at their hands.

"Friend, what troubles you? Why the wailing?" came a voice from the darkness. A tall, swarthy chap stepped into the glimmer of light thrown off by the man's small fire.

"I'm lost and I fear myself and my trusty dog will perish if we cannot find the famed oasis that we seek. The poor creature can barely stand he is so thirsty and I am sure he is not long for this world. I blame myself for all this."

"Why do you not give some of your water to the dog? I see you have a large skin full."

"Because I might need the water myself," replied the tribesman!

We might apply this story to our own lives and indeed the wide world. A world where some have more than they need and others have none or nothing! Have we ever seen someone using a small piece of soap in the shower knowing we have three bottles of our own, or hoarded clothing or food knowing others have little or nothing? People talk of famine in parts of the world – yet even with the largest population that there has ever been on Earth, we grow enough food to feed all – if some were not so greedy!

51 THE PIZZA

I in no way wish to offend, but would like to share with you a joke that is based on religious thinking. I trust it will be read in the spirit it is offered… to educate and entertain.

A chap approached a stall selling wood-fired pizza at a festival; the smell of the cooking food drew him like a magnet. After looking at the menu board carefully, he turned to the pizza maker and said jokingly, "Can you make a Buddhist pizza?"

"Do you mean make you one with everything?" the chef asked who had obviously heard this quip before.

The man nodded and pulled a £10 note from his pocket. Soon the dough was spinning and the ingredients were placed carefully on to the base and large amounts of grated cheese were sprinkled on top. The chef slid it onto a flat wooden plate and placed it into the oven. Minutes later the bubbling pizza was slid out and cut into slices and onto a plate.

"That will be £7.50," said the chef.

The man passed his money over and the chef opened the till and placed the money inside and quickly shut the drawer.

"Oh, where's my change?" asked the man.

The pizza chef turned to him and asked, "You wanted the Buddhist pizza, didn't you?"

"Yeah, but I still expect to get my change."

"Ah, but you asked for the Buddhist pizza and should therefore know that change comes from within!"

Maybe you don't buy pizza but whatever you buy, you seek and expect change, as do we all. But we all need to realise that the most important changes come from within us. When we change our values, ideas, plans, expectations and desires, these changes can only happen if within us there is the motivation and will to be different and, indeed, be better!

52 THE RIVER CROSSING

One day, four devotees of a highly respected teacher were stood at a river bank thinking about crossing over. The current was strong and the water was deep and very cold. They were all very apprehensive. The water swirled and fizzed around a number of rocks that stuck up above the water's surface... the crossing did look perilous. The devotees had heard many people had drowned and that the crossing was dangerous.

They were discussing how they might make the journey when their teacher arrived. In turn, each told the teacher how they planned to cross.

"I will pray to the gods and I am sure they will guide me to shallow parts and I will safely cross," said one of them.

"I will invoke the gods to enable me to run and jump from that nearby cliff edge and glide across using my cloak as a wing and parachute," suggested a second follower.

"I will enter a trance and with my god's blessing and assistance, I will walk on the surface of the water and soon be safely on the far bank," the third set out.

Finally, the last devotee suggested he would sit and mediate until he could transform his body into its elemental particles and, with the help of the spirits of the earth and sky, his matter would be beamed across and re-assembled on the far bank!

The teacher laughed at them all and one by one dismissed their ideas as fanciful and destined to failure.

"Then how should we cross, oh wise one?" the four devotees echoed together.

"Well, you could walk fifty metres downstream to behind that large tree where you will find a boatman with a powerful outboard motor boat and ask him to take you over!"

How often have we struggled to solve a problem, or sort out an issue when it would make more sense to ask someone for their wisdom and assistance!

53 IT'S A MARMITE THING!

I was talking to someone last week who told me they didn't like Marmite! Marmite is one of those things that some people love and others hate. It is even suggested there is no in between! But maybe what is more important is those people who say they don't like it, but, when asked, they admit they have never tried it.

My mum didn't like Indian food, not that she ever tried it. My cousin doesn't like bitter beer but has never tried it. And my aunt never went on a foreign holiday because she knew she wouldn't like going abroad! This list goes on and we are all quite likely to have said or thought of something like this at some time... I wouldn't enjoy yoga... I'd never be able to learn a foreign language... I don't read science fiction, it's not my thing... I'm not a sporty person... yet have you really given these things a go?

There's a great saying: 'If you always do what you've always done, you'll always get what you've always got – if that isn't working, try anything else.'

Of course, if you have never tried something, how can you say you won't like it, enjoy it or benefit from it?

I worked for several years with a chap who every year set himself a new challenge and in six years he took up badminton, learnt Italian, walked all the footpaths with five miles of his house, took on an allotment, learnt to cook Chinese food and did an evening class in plumbing!

We might not have the opportunity to try everything but most people can listen to a new radio station, watch TV programmes that you have never watched, read a book at least every week, take up yoga, get more exercise, learn to draw or paint – the list is endless. And you can teach an old dog new tricks – you are never too old to learn – but please don't say no to anything you have not at least tried. You might discover so many different things about yourself. Of course, I persuaded the chap I was talking to to try Marmite. He loved the taste and told me his mum didn't like it so they didn't have it at home so he'd never tried it. I was of course prepared to accept he didn't like it, but not before he had tried it!

54 WHAT TO BE GOOD AT

There was once a fellow who felt he was not reaching his potential and that he was not good enough. He had a lovely wife, two delightful children, a comfortable house and a job as a teacher at his local school. He told his friends of his fears and one of them suggested he travel to far off lands to seek a holy man who would guide him. His friend had heard of this amazing teacher and, as the fellow's wife supported his quest, during the holidays he travelled to meet the holy man.

After a six-hour flight, an eight-hour train journey and a three-hour bus ride, the man arrived at a village high in the hills in a remote part of a remote land. After a restless, yet excited, night in a hotel, he set off at dawn to walk the six hours to meet the teacher. The path was uneven and as he climbed it got colder and he found the altitude made him breathless. As the light began to fade, he arrived at a cave high on the hillside. At the cave entrance sat a devotee of the holy man and the man explained that he sought all the wisdom he needed to be as good as he could be. The devotee told him many people came to gain this teaching and that he should sleep under the rugs at the cave entrance and at dawn the master would speak with him. After such a demanding journey he was soon asleep and, although the ground was uncomfortable, he slept well.

He awoke early and was keenly anticipating the great wisdom from the teacher. He anticipated ancient texts and books to study, practices to practice and devotions to undertake. He imagined he might need to mediate, pray, read, chant and maybe even undergo fasting or some form of cleansing. He had made plans to stay several weeks here if he needed to, in order that he might become as good as he could.

The first light came over the hillside opposite the cave entrance and lit up the cavern behind him. The smell of incense wafted from within and a voice called him to enter and pay his respects. The ceiling was low and he stooped to crawl along to an opening into a room where sitting on a large blue cushion was an elderly woman who beckoned to him to approach and sit with her. She asked him to explain why he had come and what sort of life he lived. After listening carefully, she looked into the man's eyes and said, "You must go home as quickly as you can and when you get there and, only when you do, open the envelope that I will give you and read it."

The man took the envelope and with great intrigue set off to go back home. Three days later he stepped back into his home where his wife and family welcomed him – surprised that he was back so soon.

"Where's the envelope?" they all cried with excitement and anticipation.

He tore it open and read: 'True goodness cannot come from following a teacher, a holy book or worshiping anything… it comes from being the best you can at what you are!'

And from that day forth, the man sought to be the best husband, father, son, neighbour and teacher that he could and he became happy and full of true goodness. So, whether you are a circus clown, a prisoner, an engineer, an office worker or a chef – be the best you can at that.

55 THE ROTTEN APPLE

Last week I went to check on the apples I had stored in the shed from the tree at the bottom of the garden. Every year the tree is loaded with splendid cooking apples and at the beginning of October we pick them and store them in large trays for use over the winter. Each week we check the apples and each week there are one or two that are rotten or have started to rot. These we take out of the trays and use the good bits to make pies and crumbles. One of this week's apples had completely rotted and all that was left was a brown soggy mess in the paper it had been wrapped in. My daughter suggested it was useless and was set to throw it into the compost bin. She suggested it was a pointless waste for an apple to rot so completely, and that it was a bad bit of evolution for an apple to be so likely to rot that it would be made useless by rotting like this.

I reminded her that if rotting did not happen, the earth would be covered in apples, other fruit and leaves, and, of course, fungi were also part of evolution and had evolved to live on this vegetative material. By rotting the material, fungi were returning nutrients to the soil from where plants could once more use them to grow... thus a cycle was complete. I told her to take the rotting apple in the garden and break it apart carefully and see what was inside. She returned with eight seeds or apple pips. These pips, I told her, are the means by which new apple trees could grow, thus the tree could reproduce itself. And what's more, the rotting flesh of the apple would enrich the soil where the pips fell giving the seeds the best start next year.

I have heard prison referred to by people as a rotting hell hole! And maybe this rotting is not so bad after all. Maybe like the apple, the rotting of the old person, or at least parts of the old person, can enrich the new life that can grow out of the seeds of opportunity that lie inside us all! And like the apple, it is only by the old lifestyle rotting that a new one can grow in the future! But like the apple we need to focus upon the seeds of our life that can grow into whatever – just as the pips can grow into new trees once the old ways or fruit has rotted away.

56 BAD STUDENTS, GOOD TEACHER!

I once worked as a teacher in a secondary school with over nine hundred students and each year I would have several classes of students to work with and to prepare for examinations. And every year the success of the students would vary – most would do well, some would do very well and a few less well. One day I sat and asked my colleagues what it was that made the difference.

One colleague told me that if the group of students do particularly well it is because you are a great teacher and if they do particularly badly it is because they were a particularly bad group of students. This comment was met with approval from a number of colleagues although it seemed rather unreasonable and unlikely to be true. The colleague added that the exam board had a quota of who could pass, so if students at other schools did well or better than ours, more of ours would do badly. Indeed, one tutor even suggested this was why they had failed their driving test. He claimed the driving examiners have a quota each month and once they have passed this number, everyone else fails! There are of course many factors that influence performance, and ability and aptitude matter as does the quality of the teachers. Hopefully the assessment is based upon criteria that means all can pass or all can fail!

Assessment based upon criteria means that passing

depends upon meeting criteria and not luck with numbers! And let us hope the staff that work with us are all great teachers and instructors – because those that guide, inform and facilitate our learning can get great results from all of us. But woe betide us if the teachers put our failure down to it being our fault and label us as useless no goods just because we have offended! A teacher or instructor and boss can help us grow, learn and create if they are great.

57 THE LIMPET

There was once a large limpet that lived on a rock at a beautiful coastal headland. The limpet had attached to the spot as do all these shellfish, who – like snails, cockles and mussels – get their food from the rock they attach to and from the sea water washing over them.

The limpet had been in the same spot for over a year and whilst it did move around a bit during high-water, it always returned to the same spot when the tide went out.

In recent months the limpet had got increasingly irritated. A number of new limpets had attached themselves nearby and they did not always respect where the limpet rested each day and occasionally, he had to flex his muscles and move on intruders. The seaweed that grew on the rocks had done well in the warm summer sun and when the tide was high, the weed got washed about and kept brushing into the limpet which also irritated him. And to make matters worse, the rocks were being invaded by barnacles that grew quickly and were taking up all the free space on the rocks.

One afternoon when the tide was high, a small fish was swimming around and as it approached the limpet it paid its respects and asked if it could search for scraps of food around the base of the shell. The limpet was happy to agree and delighted that the fish was so respectful that he thanked it and even spat out a few bits of food it had scraped off the rocks that it had saved for itself. The fish ate them and thanked the limpet and asked it how things were. The fish almost wished it hadn't asked as the limpet set forth and bent the fish's ear about all that the limpet saw that was wrong about where it lived.

The fish listened carefully and politely. After the limpet had finished, it said, "Why don't you move?"

The limpet replied it had always lived there and feared it might be worse somewhere else.

"You won't know unless you try," said the small fish.

Having had a particularly irritating time with the new limpets, barnacles and seaweed, the limpet set off. It soon found a spot a good distance from its old home and attached itself. Three weeks later it was surprised to see the small fish, who greeted it, asking how things were.

"Brilliant. There's no seaweed always in my face and no troublesome neighbours and plenty of food on the water currents that flow here. I wish I'd moved sooner, thank you so much."

To what extent do we have a mindset like that limpet? The rut we are in is actually not that good, but it's what we know and we are fearful that if we move and/or change, we might not like the alternative. We will never know till we try! For many people, life is not the best… but they are stuck in a rut. And if that is you, it may be time for a change!

58 THE FISHERMAN

A man sat one day at a river bank, casting his rod and line into the sparkling waters of the river, hoping to catch fish for supper for his family. He carefully threw ground bait out into the water and cast his line so the baited hook drifted under the bank at the far side of the stream where the water ran slow and deep. This, he thought, would be the best place to catch something. But nothing, and after thirty minutes he decided the shallow part of the river would be better where the water bubbled and was full of oxygen so he cast his line there. And still not even a bite boosted his hopes.

So, he packed up and decided to return in the evening when maybe the fish would want something to eat. If necessary, he decided to stay into the night, thinking that maybe in the daylight the fish could see him and were put off by his presence.

That day he caught nothing but undeterred he returned the following day and used different bait and tried the same places and times of the day… still he caught nothing.

On the third day he returned once more again with different bait, determined to try in the same places and at all the same times. After a few minutes, a man came by and asked him how he was getting on. He told him it was a useless place to fish as he had caught nothing in three days and was getting very hungry.

The man sat next to him and said it was strange that he had caught nothing as they could both see plenty of big fish swimming in the clear waters. The man asked him if he ever fell out with people or got into arguments. He thought this was an odd question, but said that of course he did because people often talked nonsense in his opinion and when they did, he saw to it that they were put right! He even agreed that other people would ignore the nonsense spouted by others but he could not resist a scrap.

The man asked if him if he saw the connection with fishing and he quickly answered no.

"The two are very different," he retorted.

"Not at all," said the man. "In life we get thrown a great deal of bait – people pick a fight, try and wind us up and even talk nonsense – but it is up to us whether we take the bait. You have done nothing wrong in your fishing. Indeed you have been wise to offer the fish as much variety as you could, but they just aren't biting."

Learn this in life… if you find you are forever getting into fights, whether verbal or even physical, perhaps it is because you take the bait.

59 THE JIGSAW

Tom was sitting one day, carefully doing a jigsaw puzzle and was irritated when a friend interrupted him.

"It's about life itself, it's the most important thing in my life," he said, making it clear why he was carefully placing the pieces on the board.

Eventually Tom stopped and went off to do something else.

The friend looked carefully at the picture... it was of a scene in the country, any country, with a small river running by a cottage, a snowy mountain range in the background and a field of grazing cows in the foreground. The friend looked all over the box to see where the picture was from, thinking it must be where Tom had been born, or maybe where he lived as a child. But as far as he could tell it was not a real place. Maybe it was a home Tom had wished or dreamt of, or contained all the things he had wanted from life but had not got.

The next day Tom was once more busy at the table doing a jigsaw. His friend leant over his shoulder to see the picture and once more Tom told him to leave and let him focus on this special task. The picture was of a cathedral and some water meadows and the friend thought maybe Tom had deep faith and wanted to be alone to talk with the Almighty.

Most days of the week Tom would spend some time

working on a jigsaw and, when not working on them, carefully rolled them up on a mat so he could continue them at any time. The picture seemed unimportant and Tom would get puzzles from the library and seemed to always have at least one on the go. Eventually the friend had to ask Tom why were jigsaws were so important to him.

"They are a representation of life – as long as you have the corners and indeed most of the outside edges you can tackle whatever is in the middle! My corners in life are my partner, my dad, my son and my best friend, and whilst I have those four corners, I can do anything! The rest of the edges are the constants that I have in place, like the experiences I value, the books I enjoy, the music I love and the friends I have made. My life at the moment is like the centre of the jigsaw – all over the place and chaotic and disorganised, but with the corners and border I can work on all that and in time I will get the picture sorted. Like all puzzles it takes time, but as long as you have those corner and edge foundations, you have a great stating place."

So, get thinking and get sorting. What are your corner pieces and what makes the edges of your life? Once you establish these foundations, you can move forward.

60 FLIES OR BEES

The teacher stood in front of her class of thirty students and asked them which animals are more intelligent, flies or bees. The class thought about the question and each one in turn answered bees. They gave a number of reasons: bees build a sophisticated home and make honey, bees have a clear social order, bees help us and themselves by pollinating flowers… flies eat rotting material and dung, flies come from horrible maggots and flies spread diseases. It was clear why all the class chose bees over flies.

The teacher then held up a small glass cylinder the size of a drinks can and inside she put three bees and three flies. She placed one open end against the window glass in the room and the other was open into the room and she told the students to watch the glass cylinder carefully. The six insects started flying around and quickly the three bees moved to the window end of the tube and started flying against the window glass. The flies seemed to behave more randomly but soon one of them reached the open end of the cylinder and escaped into the room. The three bees continued to bang against the window glass and were soon seen to be tiring and flying less actively. The two other flies also found the open end and flew off into the room. The teacher asked the students to explain what had happened and think through their answers about whether bees or flies are more intelligent.

More than half the students changed their minds and decided the flies were brighter – after all, they had escaped the tube and had the teacher not stopped the experiment, the bees would still be banging their heads against the glass. The bees are of course attracted to one thing… the sun, and it was their attempts to get to the sun that led them to fly at the window. Flies on the other hand are less single minded, very inquisitive and seek out new options and opportunities everywhere.

Now the question that really matters is whether you are a bee or a fly. Do you pig-headedly carry on behaving in a way that gets you nowhere? Or like the flies, are you open-minded and prepared to seek opportunities and options wherever and whenever?

61 CHANGE

A man took over a business from his father when dad decided to retire and was soon thinking about what needed changing. He had heard the sayings, 'a new broom sweeps' and 'out with the old', so he set about making changes to their suppliers, distribution systems, working practices and many other aspects of the business. After all, he had been to university and studied business management. The business only made a small profit and he thought there were many untapped markets and opportunities.

He had heard about streamlining, maximising returns and optimising returns whilst studying and felt dad had let the business fall behind competitors and was rather old fashioned. What he suggested looked good on paper and he managed to persuade the board of directors that a number of things should change.

The changes were made and after only a few weeks, unrest began to appear amongst the staff and the customers, and soon profits started to fall. In desperation he went to see a guru – not of business, but at a temple, where the guru taught people and not business. The guru told the man a story of what it was like when he had become the master at the temple. He felt the daily routine was not the best, the robes the monks wore were not to his liking and some of the practices were not those he was used to and he thought change was needed.

Before making any changes, he decided to spend a week meditating on the issue and one afternoon he went to the monastery kitchen to see that lunch was nearly ready. Stirring a big pot was a delightful lady who for years had supported the monks and who came every day to help cook lunch.

"Taste this, master," she said. "I think it would be improved by more spice. What do you think?"

The guru stopped in his tracks and ran from the kitchen exclaiming, "Improvement!"

And that, the guru said to the business man, must be your mantra: not what needs changing but what needs improvement.

The businessman returned to his workplace, gathered a large group of staff around him and asked them what should and could be improved. After listening carefully, he again made changes but only if they would bring about improvement. Soon the business started to grow and before long it became a market leader; with everyone gaining from the changes.

We should all remember this simple mantra – all improvement requires change but not all change is improvement!

62 WHICH WAY DO YOU FACE?

After struggling for years with his 'nerves', a chap met a wise teacher. The man had suffered bouts of depression, had made little of his life and for a long time had felt sad and very low. He had tried everything: exercise routines, tablets, counsellors, doctors and all manner of therapists. He was at the end of his tether and took himself to the end of the beach cliff with thoughts of throwing himself into the sea. As he reached the end of the cliff path, he was put off jumping as there was an elderly lady sitting on a bench staring out to sea. He decided to sit at the opposite end of the bench to wait for her to leave.

After a few minutes she stood up and he sensed his time was near at hand. Instead of leaving, she moved along the bench and sat next to him and spoke.

"Hello friend, you look as if you carry the troubles of the world," she exclaimed.

"Where do I start? My two wives both left me, and I have three children who will have nothing to do with me, I've been in prison more years than out in the last fifteen years, I drink too much and I have no job, no home and no hope," he sobbed. "I failed at school, my dad beat me and I have nothing to show for my miserable thirty five years," he continued.

"Where is the past?" the elderly lady asked him.

"Behind me and it offers little hope for what is in front of me."

"Ah, then you have things back to front. Put your past out in front of you, examine it carefully and see what you can learn from it, and keep it in mind. Now remember your future is behind you. You cannot see your future because it has not happened. However, with all you have experienced and learnt from the past you see before you, you have the wherewithal to direct the future to be very different from your past! We all sit astride a train that is hurtling along a track and unless you become a time-lord like Dr Who and can travel back in time, you cannot change any of your past. But nothing of your future is inevitable, someone might come long and push you off this cliff or come along and open a door to a new future – you never know."

Minutes later a man came along to cliff top path and greeted the woman and turned to the man. "Having a lunch break?" he asked.

The man explained he had no job and for that matter nowhere to stay and was just sitting there thinking.

"Well, if you want to get off your backside and come with me, I have work that needs doing."

Within the hour the man was digging holes for fence posts on the farmland nearby, had the promise of a place to sleep in a farm out-building and a hot meal and a bit of cash.

"I know you," said the women to the farmer standing by his truck at the cattle sales with his new wife.

"Yes, I'm that man that put his past in front and learnt from it and I have much to thank you for!"

63 THE SAT NAV

Tammy had set off from Gloucester to deliver a number of car components to Birmingham and as soon as she sat in the car turned on the radio and sat nav. After safely negotiating the outskirts of the city, she settled in to listen to the tunes and be guided by the gentle voice from her sat nav. She was making good progress until she came across roadworks to lay a new water main. The sat nav kicked in, telling her to turn at various locations and she duly followed until she drove into a farmyard.

"You are using a sat nav," said the farmer. "It thinks this is a road but from here on it's only a muddy track that my cows have turned over. Mind you, in a tractor you'd soon be on the main road!"

For many people today a vital piece of equipment in their car or other motor vehicle is a navigation system that gathers data from overhead satellites and gives an accurate indication of location and route to be taken. That said, when driving and using a device, it is important to use your own internal compass, the intuition you have from your experience as a driver to know if something is right or not. Many drivers have followed their navigation system and found themselves in a narrow country lane or driving down a dead end. Whilst the device offers a great deal of assistance, you should always combine it with your internal compass; a compass that says this road is too narrow or has rarely been used – maybe it's wrong? At that point you should stop and check to avoid making a mistake that takes time and effort to resolve.

The same is true about advice and guidance from other people… whoever they are. When you hear a teaching, listen to advice or get directions from anyone, always refer to your inner compass because if it doesn't seem right, it probably isn't! When that helpful person you meet offers you advice or opinions, always proceed with caution – your inner compass will say 'take care' even if your stomach and eyes say a big yes please!

No one minds you asking for time to think things over and often a bit of thought allows that inner compass to protect you from acting foolishly. At some point you might apply for a job or maybe you will be responsible for choosing a candidate or needing to make a decision in life. The skills we look for or should demonstrate are: head (intellectual skill), hands (practical skill), heart (emotional skill) and of course hari! As in hari kiri – to spear yourself in the guts – your gut reaction, or inner compass, should always help guide you. Learn to listen to that inner voice that says be cautious, say no or check again.

64 CAN A DONKEY BE A COW?

There was once a donkey who lived on a farm along with a number of other animals. Every day he looked over into the field of cows and was envious; they all looked so calm and majestic and gracefully wandered around the field eating all day. The donkey lived in a rather tired old paddock with little grass and no company, so one evening he pushed over the old fencing and followed the cows into the high pasture.

As he followed the herd, he said to himself, "Now I'm a cow as well, I'm in the cows' field, following other cows and eating the grass that cows eat, so I must be a cow!"

A little after, a crow perched on the donkey's back and asked him what he was doing and once more he asserted he was a cow because he was with cows doing what cows do. The crow put the donkey right, telling him that just because he mixed with cows didn't make him a cow. The crow told the donkey that only the day before a group of pilgrims had passed through the farm; there were twelve pilgrims, all devout holy people full of grace and goodness and they were accompanied by many people from the village. "But," said the crow, "only the pilgrims were truly devout and virtuous – just by following pilgrims doesn't make you a pilgrim!"

It's like going to the gym every day or attending education sessions… just being there does not make you fit and healthy or educated and skilled! You have to get fully involved, commit yourself to hard work and truly change yourself. Like the donkey, you can be where the cows are but that does not make you a cow. Just by mixing with people will not change you or make you like them; that only comes with hard work with your mind and body.

65 TWO ENVELOPES

A man lay on his death bed and as the end approached, his only son came to say goodbye. The man had lived well and welcomed the end of his life as he was now very old and not in the best of health. His son was sad but was able to tell his dad how much he loved him and to thank him for all the support and help he had given as a father. The old man reached under his pillow and pulled out two envelopes and gave them to his son.

"These will guide you through life without me. When you hit rock bottom and fear there is no longer any point to life – open an envelope for guidance and when you hit the heights of success, open the other one!"

Puzzled by this gesture, the son put the envelopes in his pocket and soon after, his father died. The son was busy arranging and leading the celebration of his father's life and forgot the two envelopes.

Many years later, the man found himself destitute! His business had collapsed, his wife had left him and he discovered he needed to have a major operation. He sat in his garden thinking about things and realised he had never felt so low, when he remembered his dad's envelopes. He went inside the house and found his old jacket and there in the pocket were the two envelopes. He took one out and opened it in eager anticipation of what it might say.

Written in the scrawled hand of his father were the words: 'This will pass!'

The man sat and thought about this and it indeed offered him some comfort. Three months later he had successfully had treatment and was fully recovered, an old business partner asked him to join his company and he got a better job than he had before, and a wonderful woman had come into his life.

Years went by and he sat one day in his new garden – he had moved into this splendid new home, he was now the owner of a big successful company and was able to help many other people get good work and he and his new partner had three beautiful children. What could be better, he thought, and then he remembered what his father had said and he went to the kitchen where hanging behind the door was his old jacket. He took the second envelope from the pocket and opened it in eager anticipation of what it might say. Written in the scrawled hand of his father were the words: 'This will pass!'

He smiled and went back to his new garden with clear understanding of the way things always were and always will be – ever changing as they will be in all our lives.

66 THE CONCENTRATION CAMP

The men had been held in the concentration camp for many months. They saw little hope of escape and many had become very thin and were in poor health. The war had been long and many people had been killed. Many more taken captive and held in camps such as this.

The guards demanded work from the inmates and treated everyone harshly. Each day the men were taken out to work the frozen ground with basic tools and no warm clothing. The huts were cold and the thin blankets did little to keep out the cold, the beds harboured bed bugs and were were crudely made from wood. The men used dried vegetation to provide some softening as they had no mattresses.

The days were cold outside and at this time of the year the weather was often grey and overcast, and the nights were colder. The men had only the ragged clothes they stood in and had few comforts and no contact with the outside world. The food was very poor and each day the only meal was watery soup that was served with stale bread that was so hard it had to be dipped into the soup.

Yet still there were men in the camp that walked through the huts comforting others, giving away their last crust of stale bread. There were few of these generous individuals but they offered proof that you can take everything from a person except one thing… the last of all freedoms – the freedom to choose how you respond to a situation.

Life does not always treat us well and at times we suffer; although I hope you don't have to cope with a rough and hard bed, poor food and inferior lifestyle to that which you are used to or desire. However tough your life is or aspects of it have become, no one can take away your freedom to respond to it with a positive frame of mind.

67 THE OLD VIOLIN

One afternoon at the auction room, a violin came up for sale. It was evidently old and looked rather battered, and it came in a case with a bow. Before the bidding could begin, the auctioneer's assistant was tasked with playing the instrument. Hesitantly he held up the instrument, scratched the bow over the strings and produced a dreadful sound.

"Well, what am I bid for this fine old instrument," the auctioneer asked.

The bidding began: £15, £20, £25 at which point the auctioneer felt the reserve price would not be reached and he would not get much commission.

"Surely it is worth more and surely someone can make this instrument truly sing," he declared.

At that point an elderly woman from the crowd came forward and took the violin and bow. She dusted the body and neck of the violin with her handkerchief, tightened the bow and tuned the strings. She then played a tune that made everyone stop and listen.

After she stopped playing, she handed the instrument back to the assistant and the auctioneer picked up his gavel and once more invited bids.

"Now, I'm sure that will put a different perspective on this fine instrument," he said as a bid of £1000 was made. Another of £1500 was quickly followed by £2000 and eventually the gavel fell at £28,000. The crowd cheered the price that was reached but someone called out, "How come the worth has changed so much?"

"Clearly it was the touch of the hand of an expert that has revealed the true value of the violin," said the auctioneer.

As it is in our lives, many of us have lives that are out of tune – the tune we play sounds scratchy, unappealing, unattractive and does not do us justice. What then if an expert teacher, mentor or guide was to take the rather shabby individual we have become and guide us to achieve, then maybe like that old violin we would play a different tune and increase our value.

68 THE GOLDEN BUDDHA

One afternoon, one of the monks at a Buddhist temple made a discovery. For years they had focused their practice on a large, rather dull, grey stone statue at the front of their temple. The statue had been given to the monks to safeguard in the temple for fear that an invading army might desecrate it. The monks were sure the invaders would respect the holy site and indeed long after the war was over and the invaders retreated, they continued to use the statue as the centrepiece of their worship and practice.

As the years went by, on several occasions, the community offered to buy the monks a splendid new metallic statue that would make their temple look glorious. The monks refused, in part because the money would be better be spent on the local community, building and maintaining a school and health centre. After years of commenting, the community managed to persuade the monks to allow the mediation hall to be upgraded to accommodate more people even if the old grey statue was to remain. The community were surprised to find the concrete statue was remarkably heavy and as it was being moved it toppled over and the concrete cracked at the side. To everyone's amazement, it was realised the statue only had a thin coat of concrete to cover the solid gold statue that lay beneath; a statue worth £200million weighing 5.5 tons that can be seen today in a temple in Thailand.

Whilst this is an amazing story what it offers to each of us is the importance of seeing below the current exterior to what might lie beneath. When you look around the people you come across in everyday life, you might see a crowd of individuals strutting and posturing to save face in a challenging world. A world where dishonesty, back-biting, gossip and harsh behaviour arises. Underneath this are so often people who feel insecure, uncertain and lacking in self-worth or self-confidence. What so many of us need to do is to chip away that hardened exterior shell and see what lies beneath – it may not be solid gold but it will so often be worth so much more than we have on display at present.

69 PANDORA'S BOX

Many of us have heard the phrase, 'You've opened Pandora's box' – meaning to let all sorts of bad things loose onto the world or a situation. In the classic story, Zeus, the god, gave newlywed Pandora the gift of a locked box that came with a note that said: 'DO NOT OPEN.' Which was very odd, but as you would guess Pandora was very curious and, unable to resist temptation, she decided to open the box. As she lifted the lid, out flew all the bad things in the world today: envy, sickness, hate, greed and disease. Pandora tried desperately to close the lid, but it was too late. She showed the box to her husband… it was now empty, except for one thing that then escaped – hope! The hope that would make all the difference in the world in the face of all the bad things she had let loose.

Hope is an interesting word… one we should all think about more often and one we should try and put to work in our lives. For most people in custody, they should work on the hope that one day they will leave prison and make a new live – one they hope will be better. For gardeners, there is the hope that this year there will be less pests, more rain, more sun and better crops. For the musician, hope that this year will bring more concerts, better album sales and that all elusive hit record. Having that hope should encourage us all to build for a better tomorrow – wherever that tomorrow might be.

I hope that tomorrow I will manage my fears more constructively, I will use my time more wisely, I will resist all that food I like but that is bad for me and I will find the enthusiasm to get more exercise. If we all list the things we hope for tomorrow and indeed in the future, short and long term, we can then work on getting those hopes to happen. We all experience the envy, sickness, hate, greed and disease that Pandora let loose on the world but some of us fail to realise that she also let hope loose. Life is not always a bed of roses and in our darkest moments – and we all get them – remember what Eleanor Roosevelt said, "No one can devalue you without your consent." Stand up for yourself and remember, without favouring one Liverpool football team over another: with hope in your heart, you'll never walk alone! Walk with hope as your constant life companion – hope that will enable you to make each day better, to get the most out of each moment in time and hope that your future will be better than your present and past. It was hope that kept so many prisoners of war and victims of torture going, surviving extremely demanding situations by keeping hope alive.

70 THE MANAGER

A month ago, I was taken by a friend to have lunch in a small restaurant. The food was Sri Lankan and, as we had not eaten there before, we asked the waiter if he would help us choose. He carefully talked through the menu and explained what each dish was and cautioned us about eating anything too spicy.

The meal soon arrived and indeed there were many ingredients in dishes we had not eaten before and many new flavours. The food was similar to much Indian subcontinent food, but at the same time very different. Even the rice was different. We had two types: one much shorter than we were used to and with an earthy smell, the other flavoured with coconut. In fact, a good deal of coconut had been used in many of the dishes and one we really enjoyed was called a hopper which came with a fried egg in it! We enjoyed the main course and asked for a traditional pudding. We were recommended a dish called wattalapan. It was sweet, creamy and nutty... a wonderful end to the meal!

Overall, the meal was great and we even felt we would happily have paid more for it! The surroundings were clean and cheerful and it was decorated with country scenes from Sri Lanka which made for a delightful lunch. And all at a very reasonable price.

Just before we left, I called a waiter over and asked

if the manager was available. He looked concerned and asked if there was anything wrong with our meal and disappeared to the kitchen. A few minutes later he returned as we had asked him to bring our bill and as I paid for the food I again asked if the manager was free. He looked concerned again and asked if we were not happy with the food. We assured him we were delighted. No manager came but as we were about to leave, a gent in a suit emerged from the kitchen door and I went over to speak to him. The waiter looked on extremely anxious from the kitchen door. I told the manager we had really enjoyed our meal and to thank his staff and that the waiter had been exceptionally helpful. He thanked us for feeding this back and we left.

My friend turned to me and said how surprised they had been that the waiter looked so anxious. "Maybe no one has ever paid him a compliment before," he queried.

I suggested it is quite likely and said I always thanked people for good service and liked to let the manager know when their staff had done a great job. Maybe we are all too quick to moan and complain but maybe we should go out of our way to give praise where it is due. Someone told me one day that for every word of praise a young person gets, they get ten moans! Start today by making sure for each time you moan about someone or something, you balance it by offering thanks, praise or encouragement to someone else.

71 THE POT PLANTS

A number of years ago, university researchers carried out an experiment with the residents in a care home. Half the residents were given a small simple pot plant to look after and the other half were not! Those with a pot plant clearly showed an interest in it and even if they were unable to water it themselves, they made sure one of their carers or visitors did. Most of the plants thrived. This was no surprise to the researchers as they had expected the pot plants that were carefully looked after would do well. What did surprise them was the life expectancy and importantly the quality of life of the plant owners was significantly better than for those that had no plant!

Being occupied, having responsibility and having a plant to care for gave those residents a sense of purpose and a reason to be, and the researchers found these residents did more and got much more out of life, as well as reporting a higher sense of well-being on assessment tests.

You may not be able for some reason to keep a pot plant, but we can all seek out purposeful activity to enhance the quality of our life. Most people can find work opportunities, even if it is only voluntary work at first. Volunteering can lead to paid work. Most people can do something by way of exercise, go to the library and learn to love learning. You don't need to go on a formal course at an institution, we can all learn from books, the internet, radio and TV. We can all listen to educational radio programmes or change our TV viewing habits to watch documentaries. I appreciate not all opportunities are available for everyone but most people have a range of things they can do that are purposeful. You might even be allowed a pot plant or get a chance to grow vegetables or flowers. And whilst you might say you cannot see the point in maybe living longer, this might change with getting a better quality of life.

72 TULIP BULBS

My dad went to Holland eighteen months ago and brought back with him a big sack of tulip bulbs. He gave half to me and half to my brother. We both planted our bulbs and waited patiently over winter to see what they would produce. Dad was keen to see the results and in March this year he visited my brother and I over the same weekend, in part to inspect our tulips. He carefully took photographs and asked us about our growing methods.

The following weekend he invited both families to lunch and had made a poster of the two tulip 'crops'. My brother's tulips were patchy; some were tall and full of colour and some rather short with small uninteresting flowers. In total, my brother had fifty-six tulips in bloom. I had ninety-four blooms and all but a couple were in full colour with luxurious foliage and big flower heads.

Dad said, "Now it is clear which one of you got the best results and just to make sure you were competing on even terms I must tell you… mother mixed the bulbs and chose which ones went into which bag then you chose which bag we should each have."

My brother had been busy when he first got the bulbs and so planted them three weeks after me. He threw them randomly over a piece of the garden and planted them where they landed then because he got a new job at the end of last year, he forgot about them until he was reminded that they would be inspected in March.

I chose a part of the garden that got good sunlight and dug in some manure from the chickens before I planted each one about nine inches down in the ground, making sure they had reasonable space between them.

Just like tulips, our own bodies are more likely to bear good fruit or good results if we are carefully looked after. If we eat well, get plenty of exercise, sleep wisely and avoid dangerous habits we will do better. The individual who smokes spice, drinks hooch, eats junk food, gets no exercise and goes to bed at any time and gets up whenever, will do much less well than the person who avoids intoxicants, eats wisely, goes to the gym and sleeps seven to eight hours each night. It is a sad fact that homeless people have a life expectancy that is under fifty, brought on mainly by their lifestyle. Moderate obesity, which is now common, reduces life expectancy by about three years, and severe obesity can shorten a person's life by ten years… a ten-year loss is equal to the effects of lifelong smoking! And whilst quantity of life may be less important to you – good living gives a better quality of life!

73 THE OLD LION

After many years of hunting for food and providing for his family, the old lion decided he should teach his offspring how to hunt for themselves. He took the three cubs to the edge of the rocky outcrop where they lived to a vantage point over the plains where the antelopes and wildebeests fed. As they approached the spot from where they got the best view, he explained the importance of progressing slowly and containing your urge to dash at the first animal you saw.

Before he had finished his words, the first cub rushed out onto the plains as soon as he saw a grazing prey animal. The whole herd of animals fled before the cub could get anywhere near them and he caught nothing but a face full of dust and dirt.

The old lion roared to the cub to come back and after an excited scamper on the plain, the cub returned empty handed with its tail between its legs.

The old lion told the cubs they should lay low and wait for the animals to return and this time do as he had said. The cubs settled down and watched and waited and slowly the grazing animals returned to the plain.

At the front of the herd was a large and impressive male antelope who soon settled to eat the scrubby grass. Unable to contain his excitement, another of the cubs launched himself off the rocks towards this mighty beast, roaring and slashing his paws. The animal quickly turned and accelerated away leaving the cub alone without the precious kill that he desired.

Once again, the old lion roared at this cub and the youngster retreated to the rocks, where, like his sibling he was dressed down by the old lion. The old lion told the three cubs to stay right where they were and wait.

Once the grazing animals had returned, the old lion explained several things – first, you need to get much closer and to launch your attack from a few metres away and not plunge off the rocks. Second, you need to approach in silence. Third, we will attack a chosen animal in formation. After carefully explaining the strategy, the four lions slowly and silently crept down from the rocks until they surrounded the herd and were in place to attack the elderly wildebeest that the old lion had chosen. In a swirl of dust, the four lions rushed in from four directions and soon had their prey on the ground and subdued. That day the lions all ate well and had learnt important lessons.

Important lessons we might all learn: to work together with others on challenging tasks, carefully and deliberately approach challenges and don't just rush at things without thinking. Listen to the wisdom of your elders and choose your target and choose the battles you fight to improve your chance of success.

74 WHAT TO LEARN

One afternoon, a ferryman was taking a passenger across a river. The river was wide, deep and very fast flowing, and clearly the only way to cross was on his boat. He only had one passenger… a lecturer at a nearby college who was going out into the countryside to gather rock samples for his studies.

"Best hold on, water's rough 'ere. Wouldn't wanna drown," said the boatman as the scholar took his seat on the ferry.

The boat was soon in mid-stream and the water was beginning to come over the side and fill the boat. As the boatman struggled to handle the boat and was beginning to panic that the boat might sink, the scholar turned to him and rather bluntly asked him if he had ever studied grammar as he was startled at how the boatman had spoken to him. The boatman explained he had not had much time for books and the like, and was a simple fellow. The scholar tuned to the boatman and rather scornfully said to him, "My fellow, never studied! Then half of your life has been wasted!"

As the boatman continued to wrestle with the boat, fearing it might capsize, he turned to the passenger and asked, "Have you ever learned how to swim?"

"No. Why would I want to do something like that? There are much more important things for a person to learn and understand, like astrology, geology and the sciences," replied the scholar.

The boatman then turned to the scholar and replied, "Then I guess as you've learnt nothing practical then all your life has been wasted... we are sinking!"

We should all widen our learning to include life-skills and practical skills, as well as the more academic things.

75 THE TRIBAL MASK

Albert visited the antique shop one afternoon, in part to shelter from the heavy rain that was falling that afternoon. He travelled for work and was in the town to see one of his less valuable customers. The shopkeeper welcomed him and told him to ignore the prices on things as he would always negotiate the price and was keen to sell everything and anything in the shop. Albert spent an hour wandering round the large shop but nothing really caught his eye until he noticed a rather odd tribal mask hanging on a wall.

He approached the shopkeeper and, despite his requests, and indeed protests, the man refused to state a price for the mask and said it was the only thing that was not for sale.

A month later Albert was back in the town and, as well as seeing his reluctant customer to try and drum up more business, he wanted to check if the mask had been sold. He returned to the shop and went straight to the place where the mask hung and it was still there. He sought out the shopkeeper and again asked if the mask was for sale. The shopkeeper told him everything in the shop had a price and a price that could be negotiated, except the mask, which was not for sale. Albert left unhappy and went to his customer.

Over the next few weeks, he felt drawn to the mask and

kept thinking about it and why the shopkeeper wouldn't sell it. Instead of waiting a month, Albert returned to the town two weeks later and went straight to the shop. He again sought out the shopkeeper and again asked if the mask was for sale. The shopkeeper told him everything in the shop had a price and a price that could be negotiated. Albert asked if that included the mask and the man told Albert to follow him. They went to where the mask was hung and the shopkeeper told Albert it was priced at £200 but he could have it for £50.

Albert was delighted and quickly handed over the money.

"Why did you refuse to sell me the mask before and why now have you sold it to me so cheaply?" Albert enquired.

"It's a very beautiful and sacred object that I was only prepared to sell to someone that really wanted it and would care for it. I had to be sure you were genuine in your interest. The fact you have come three times tells me you really want the mask and I admire your tenacity."

Whilst in the town Albert once again called on the reluctant customer.

"Well, you're nothing but persistent," said the customer. "And given your perseverance with me, I have decided to move much of my business to you and increase my dealing with you by 1000%."

Albert was delighted and drove home with a broad grin on his face at getting the mask and gaining so much new business. He stopped half way home to get fuel for his car and a cup of coffee. As he sat drinking his coffee, it dawned on him that what had got him these two successes was persistence – that sense of never giving up to get something he wanted – a sense I hope you have! Don't give up! Persistence is the key to so much success.

76 THE OLD BEAR

The three brothers sat in their mother's front room three days after she had died at the local hospital. She had been a widow for ten years and had not enjoyed the best of health in recent years and had been admitted to the hospital three weeks previously at the age of ninety-two. The sons were sad but also relieved their mother had not suffered. They met to discuss the funeral arrangements and what should happen to their mother's possessions. The house was rented and mother had left a will saying any money left after her funeral was to go to her six grandchildren, evenly divided. The sons were to divide the contents as they thought fit.

The eldest said he should have her jewellery as he was her first next of kin! The second son said he would take the cabinet of valuable cut glass, leaving nothing of value for the third son, Amos.

"I would like to take that big old stuffed bear she kept from her childhood in the bedroom to remind me of her," Amos said.

His two brothers laughed at him behind his back, knowing they had taken advantage of his good nature.

"Well, that's settled, no going back, we are all happy with what we got from dear old mum," said the middle son, knowing he and his older brother had benefitted by goods worth hundreds, if not thousands of pounds.

The youngest son was told there were garden tools, furniture and other household goods he could sell to get some cash. The three sons rarely met and indeed the older two had little contact with the youngest brother who missed his mother, as did his wife and three children, but he had the bear to remind him of his mum.

One afternoon, his own youngest son told Amos that he should get nanny's old bear repaired as he was looking very threadbare. His wife carefully unpicked the seam at the back of the bear so she could insert more stuffing. As she did, she pulled out a small piece of paper. Written on the paper was, "Dear Amos, I know you boys so well and suspect your older brothers will have taken advantage of your good nature. To show you that you get in life what you deserve, take out all my stuffing!"

His wife carefully removed the rest of the stuffing which behind the paper note was made entirely of crumpled up £50 notes. "Well, your kindness to your mother has been rewarded, there's £4750 stuffed into the old bear along with two solid gold watches and a diamond ring," said his wife. "Mum must have known you would choose the bear to remember her by and that you would care for it by having it repaired."

In all our lives we should remember that whilst kindness may not always bring money or watches, it will always bring you good fortune!

77 BLAME THE TOOLS!

In our modern world it's not uncommon to hear the phrase, 'It's a computer error!' I recently bought a shirt online from a company, and when it arrived it was not the size I had ordered. When I contacted the company, they told me it was a mistake on their computer. They exchanged the shirt but not without me being inconvenienced. I had to get in touch with them and post the wrong shirt back before getting what I had ordered.

I ordered a meal at a fast-food restaurant last week and when it arrived the sandwich had the wrong filling, so I spoke to the chap that served me. "Oh it's a mistake on the computer!" Fortunately, I had not driven off. Had I discovered the mistake later in the day I would have ended up with a sandwich I didn't want.

Computers are, of course, machines that have to be told what to do. They have to be programmed and operated by a person. I would like to hear, "I am sorry, whoever programmed the computer must have given it the wrong instructions, or I think I might have pressed the wrong button." It's too easy to blame the machine, a machine that only did what it was told to do.

This new situation reminded me of my grandfather, who was a carpenter for all his working days and who always used the phrase, 'Measure twice, cut once.' And for whom the phrase, 'A bad workman blames his tools,' would have been so true. As a carpenter he never cut into wood – which cannot be corrected after you have cut it – unless he was sure it was the right cut. He would never say it was the saw that made the mistake, but the person using it.

So, it is true of all those people in our modern world who blame the computer – a machine – for making mistakes! In life, we all make mistakes but might learn from these two accounts about how to respond when a mistake happens. First, double check before you act to make sure what you are about to do or say is the right thing in the first place. Once you have acted, you have made the 'cut in the wood' and cannot turn back time! And if, unfortunately, you have made a mistake, don't blame the equipment or the tool, but apologise then seek to discover which person made the error and learn so the mistake is not repeated.

78 THE STRANGE TEACHER

Pierre was bored and felt he needed to do something different. On the advice of friends and family he decided to try returning to education. He'd left school at seventeen with no qualifications and felt he was in a bit of a rut. He decided to attend sessions called 'Futures' which ran each week, although he was unsure about what to expect. The session was taught by a lady who Pierre thought had 'been around the block' and had had an interesting life and an unusual accent. However, the first class did not go well for Pierre.

"Now close your eyes and imagine a caterpillar," the teacher instructed.

Pierre closed his eyes and imagined a fat green caterpillar he had once seen on a bush at his uncle's house.

"Think of the different colours on its back, the hairs on its side, the camouflaged markings and the spectacular antennae on its head."

Pierre could only think of that plain fat, green caterpillar!

"Now think of a plant, one you've never seen before. What colour is it? How tall is it? What shape and colour are the flowers and what does it smell like?"

Pierre was getting frustrated, and, as hard as he tried, all he could see was the funny red and green pot plant his dad brought home every Christmas. The plant that always died in the week after Christmas. Yet each year his dad bought one!

"Now think of a place you'd like to visit in the countryside. Describe the contours of the land, the colour of the sky and the clouds. Place trees in the landscape and imagine the different colours of green in the vegetation. Are there any birds or animals in view?"

Pierre could only think of the bit of waste ground that was behind the flats where he had been brought up and how he hated the smell of the leather factory and the rotting water in the abandoned canal! He noticed he was getting annoyed at these stupid requests and when the teacher asked for feedback on the three tasks, he was the first to put his hand up.

"It's a stupid idea! A horrid, green caterpillar, that plant my stupid dad bought each year and the dump I grew up in are not things I want to remember, let alone think about," he ranted.

Several other students in the class fed back ideas and Pierre found himself getting more annoyed as they did. Eventfully, he could listen no more and got up to leave the class. The teacher asked the class to write down the ideas they had or, if that was difficult, to draw the images and invited Pierre to come and sit at the front with her.

After a few moments, she stood up and asked the class to listen to her. "Pierre is a new student to this session and has been very helpful as he reminded me how important it is that students know why they are being asked to do something."

Pierre sat back down and noticed he was not feeling so angry.

"What I asked you to do was use your imagination because we are all victims of our past! We tend to do the things we've always done, eat the things we've always eaten, wear the clothes we've always worn, mix with the people we've always mixed with. What we should never lose sight of is doing things that are different and that require imagination. Imagine if your life was not like it is today and what would that new life be like. A famous writer once wrote, 'You are never too old to set a new goal or dream a new dream, and, if your life is not all you want it to be, you have to practice using your imagination to dream up a different life that you can become! I was once homeless and an alcoholic and I now have a home of my own, a delightful family and I haven't had a drink for ten years; all things I dreamt of in my darkest days!'

Pierre left the class resolved to work hard on his new future… as we all can, if only we can dream and imagine things that are different.

79 QUESTIONS!

Last summer, I went to a beach resort on the south coast of the country with our daughter. On our last evening, we went to the restaurant on-site to eat our evening meal. The place was crowded and I asked a family if we could join them at their table. They were very welcoming and were interested to hear how we had spent the week.

We had borrowed bikes from reception and ridden along the quiet coast road to a small secluded beach about five miles away. We had visited the nearby renovated Norman castle and had gone on the local woodland trail and zip wire experience. We had spent a day at a local craft centre making pottery objects and a driftwood picture frame, played on their crazy golf course and visited their farm visitors' centre where our daughter milked a cow!

"Dad, why did we only play on the beach each day and why didn't we do those things?" asked the young son of the family we sat with.

"Because we didn't think to ask what was available around here, and we didn't want to appear dim for not knowing," said the dad.

Last week, I spoke to a student who had not done very well in her examinations and was disappointed with her results. She was a bright student who had previously done well and had expected to be in the top 10% of the group, – but had come in the bottom 10%! We sat and discussed why she had not done very well and eventually she decided it was because she was reluctant to ask questions in class. She admitted there were often times she didn't understand what was being taught or wasn't sure what the importance was of material offered in class. She admitted to not wanting to ask questions in case it made her look stupid in front of her class mates. I reminded her it was much better to maybe appear stupid for a minute by asking the question than maybe remaining stupid for the rest of her life by not asking!

People starting a new job or moving to a new location will have many questions: where is the nearest shop? What places of interest are near here? Where is a good place to get lunch? What are my workmates or neighbours like? These and many other questions will bombard the new arrival, and some you will be able to discover or answer for yourself but never be frightened of asking.

80 THE BADMINTON MATCH

Years ago, I played a lot of badminton and one evening I turned up to play an away fixture at a club on the outskirts of town. As was usual, not all the players were there at seven o'clock; three of our team were there as I gave two other players a lift in my car. Four of our opponents were there and we decided to start with games 2 and 4 as both teams' players were present. As these players were warming up, the captain of our opponents asked me when our other players would arrive. I told him they were travelling together and would not be long. One had worked until 18.30 as a doctor at the local hospital and was playing number 5 and they would come directly from work. The first games were underway when our two missing players arrived – I nodded to them as I was refereeing one of the games in play.

"Gosh, you look too young to be a doctor," I heard the opponents' team captain announce.

"I'm not a doctor, I'm only seventeen and am still at school," I heard Greg reply.

When the first game of three ended on the court where I was refereeing, the opponents' captain came over to me. "I thought you said all your team were here."

"They are," I replied.

"I thought you said one of them is a doctor," he said, "and that they were all here."

"They are. Alison is a surgeon at the local hospital, she plays at number 5 and her son plays at number one."

He was certainly thrown to realise the doctor was female – and a surgeon at that – and when telling his colleague of his surprise, he continued to say, "But I cannot work out why they have a child playing at number one, he's only seventeen. Maybe they have put him in knowing whoever they pick will lose to our number one!"

The match was poised at two games all and the number one players' game would decide who won the match. Our opponents looked at ease as Greg took to the court and warmed up. However, their faces changed as Greg easily dispatched his opponent and we won the match. Over supper after the match, we told them Greg played for the county and for the England under-19 team and was on a national coaching squad on talented players.

What, of course, this reminds us is the importance of not judging by looks alone and the risk of making stereotyping assumptions. Not all doctors are men and many women are surgeons, and age is not the only factor to consider when judging a person's skills or abilities.

81 HELP MY SON!

One afternoon, I was travelling in a car with a friend when after a mighty clunking sound, the engine stopped. It was not obvious what was wrong so my friend called roadside assistance. Half an hour later, a rescue truck arrived. The mechanic was unable to fix the car so said he would tow us the fifteen miles to a garage near my friend's house then afterwards drop us off at his house.

I travelled in the pickup truck but my friend had to stay in his car to ensure it steered safely behind the truck. The mechanic was not very talkative, but did say, "I wonder if I'm still a waste of space!"

Once safely back at the friend's house, I told her what the mechanic had said. After a few minutes thought, she said, "Oh my word, I thought he was familiar. I sent him to prison for three months, when I was a magistrate, for non-payment of fines two years ago. I had him down as 'bad un'. Maybe I should be less hasty in labelling people!"

There is an old story told of a woman and a young man walking along a river bank. It had been raining heavily and the bank was very slippery and treacherous. The young man slipped and fell down the bank into the water. As he fell, he grabbed for a branch and managed to get hold but his body was pulled into the water. It looked as if he would be swept away in the torrent. His mother, knowing he could not swim, was fearful he would drown in the fast-flowing water, so she called out, "Help, my son, the doctor, has fallen into the water – save him!"

The villagers quickly responded and formed a human chain that entered the water and pulled the son to safety! The mother was overwhelmed with relief and thanked the villagers one by one. The son was a little shaken by the experience but not harmed in anyway.

Two elders of the village were sitting nearby and saw the event. They were delighted that no harm had come to the son. However, one turned to the other and asked, "It's interesting the woman said, 'My son, the doctor!' I wonder if the villagers would have responded so quickly had she just said her son had fallen into the water, or her son, the farm labourer."

"We will never know, but you make an interesting point. Are we all valuable, or are some more valuable that others?" the second elder asked.

During the demanding times of lockdown during the Coronavirus pandemic, we, of course, realise how important doctors are, but we also realise that refuse collectors, posties and shop workers are vital to our well-being. It's good to know the doctor was saved but we are all valuable. Each of us is unique in the world and indeed in our own world. No one can replace you or be you. Who are we to judge if a person is of worth or value?

82 THE KING

The king rode, as he did every day, to visit every corner of his beautiful mountain kingdom. On returning to the palace, he came across an apple tree that was covered in large red fruit. He stopped to pick two apples, one he gave to his horse, and the other he ate himself. The apple was sweet and crisp, and, as he bit into it, the juice ran down his chin. He had never tasted an apple that was so sweet, so he sent for his chef as soon as he got back to his palace.

"Go with three of my guards to the edge of the forest where you will find an apple tree laden with bright red fruit. Pick all the apples and bring them to the palace so we may enjoy them."

The chef and guards left immediately, but soon returned without the apples. "Sire, the tree was bare, it contained no fruit at all."

The king suspected the chef was so lazy that he had not even gone to the forest edge, so he returned there himself.

What he saw was not the tree covered in beautiful red fruit, but the poor battered remains of a tree. Every apple had been picked, and, in such haste, that many of its branches had been broken off.

The king rode back to his palace and, as he did, passed another apple tree, beautifully adorned with bright green leaves, but with no fruit. No one had touched this tree for it had no fruit, and stood in peace. The king returned to his palace where he instructed his ministers to share all of his wealth with the people of the kingdom, and to arrange for them to share in ruling the kingdom.

We might all learn from the king… if we are humble and lead a simple life it is unlikely we will be bothered by people trying to steal from us or abuse us. But if we have great wealth and we show it off, we will attract those that will seek to attack and rob us.

83 THREE SONS

Mary had been out at work all day, working as a carer in a residential home, and her husband was away working on an oil rig. She had left her three sons at home with instructions about what needed doing. Tom was seventeen, Alex fifteen and Leo thirteen, and she felt they could be trusted.

As soon as she got in, she made herself a well-deserved cup of tea and went to the cupboard to get a chocolate biscuit to have with the tea. But there were none in the cupboard, despite her knowing she had put a full packet in there only the day before! She checked the bin in the kitchen and lounge but could not find the packing from the biscuits. Eventually she went to the recycling bin in the garden and there at the top was the empty biscuit wrapper!

She called the boys down to the kitchen. Tom was keen to know what she wanted as he was planning to go out and meet friends, Alex said he was in the middle of reading a great book and Leo said he wanted to contact his best friend to get a lift to football practice.

"Before you do anything, I'd like to know where the chocolate biscuits have gone," said Mary.

The boys all denied knowing what had happened to them and each protested their innocence.

"Until you own up, the three of you are grounded and can stay here. I can wait!"

The boys all protested and told their mum it was not fair; they blamed each other and soon they were all shouting and arguing. Mary left the kitchen and said when the culprit decided to own up, she would be in the lounge drinking her tea. After half an hour, the youngest son Leo came into the room in tears. "I'm sorry, mum, it was me."

Mary went back into the kitchen with Leo and spoke to the three boys. "I am less cross about the fact that one of you took the biscuits than I am about all three of you lying. Tom and Alex, you both came into the kitchen earlier in the day and caught Leo eating the last biscuit and had even moaned at him for being so greedy. So now all three of you can help me tidy the shed before your dad gets back tomorrow."

The boys moaned that it was not fair to punish them all for Leo taking the biscuits.

"You are being punished for lying, not for taking biscuits. In life, when you make a mistake or do something wrong – own up! Had you all told the truth when I first asked, Leo could have gone to the corner shop and bought more biscuits with his own money, all three of you could have had your planned activity and I would have been happy!"

We all make mistakes in life, but not all of us are big enough to accept we are in the wrong and apologise. Indeed, we more often lie and make matters worse... as did the boys!

84 THE CROWS AND THE SNAKE

Two crows built their nest in a large tree at the edge of the forest, but, unbeknownst to them, a large snake lived in the hollowed-out trunk of the tree. The crows had spent a long time excavating their nest and felt it was an ideal spot to raise chicks. For two years the crows laid several clutches of eggs and hatched many chicks, but the snake was crafty and as soon as both parent birds left the nest, it would go to the nest and take the chicks to eat.

Eventually the crows realised what was happening and tried flying at the snake whenever they saw it. They even tried to harass it whilst it slept in the hollow tree. But after two years and no young birds to show for their efforts, the crows were on the point of seeking a new home when they decided to ask the wise owl for advice.

As advised, one of the crows went to the royal palace nearby and stole a very precious necklace belonging to the queen.

The bird carefully sat on the curtain rail in the royal bedroom, holding the necklace to be sure the queen saw him. He then flew into the palace courtyard and sat in a tree, dangling the necklace, making sure the queen and her guards saw him. He then flew off to his tree, stopping every so often on the ground to make sure the guards were coming after him.

Eventually he reached the tree where they had their nest!

On reaching the tree, the crow dropped the necklace in the tree's hollow trunk, where the snake lived. On finding the large snake, the guards pulled it from its hiding place and retrieved the necklace. Large snakes were treasured as pets by the royal household so the guards took the necklace and snake back to the palace, allowing the crows to lay eggs that this year hatched into seven handsome chicks that all left the nest.

The story, of course, reminds us all that even the most powerful enemies can be defeated with intelligence. So, in life, avoid violence and aggression to resolve differences… use wisdom instead.

85 THE LADLE

One afternoon, I heard two people taking and was surprised to hear one say, "Your trouble is, you are like a ladle."

"What do you mean?" the other man replied. "Like the big spoon in a pot of soup?"

I thought about this for a number of days and really couldn't think what he might have meant until I made some soup one evening for my family. I put a good selection of vegetables into a pot with stock and some lentils then simmered it all for thirty minutes. I had baked a loaf of bread and the smell of bread and soup brought the family eagerly to the kitchen to eat.

Just before serving it, I decided I should taste it using a big ladle and I remembered what I had overheard. The soup tasted good and the family all asked for seconds and soon the pot was empty.

One of our children then asked me a question, "Why do you use a stainless-steel ladle for soup?"

"It's our biggest spoon," said his sister.

"That is true and the size is important, but, being stainless steel, it doesn't take on the flavour of the soup so we can use it for custard and sweet things as well!" said my eldest daughter. "It goes into the soup but doesn't take up any of the flavour and is just like going to the temple or to school and not taking on board anything that you hear."

Working as a teacher I often thought to myself, I wonder what the students have learnt from being in a class. I wonder what has gone in.

As a result, I ask them, what they might do differently as a result of a workshop or class or what have they learnt today in class.

Students would usually say what they found helpful in the class, although some days some students would look back at me blankly – they were the ladles who had gone into the soup but not taken up anything! They had been in the 'soup' of the classroom and had been stirred around but none of the flavour had gone in and the ladle remained unchanged by the soup.

Remember life is like a big bowl of soup, full of interesting experiences and opportunities. But remember not to be a ladle – make sure you are changed by life's soup! And try to remember to adopt the view that I heard from a famous scientist on the radio last week, "Well, you learn something every day!"

86 BREATH

A man decided he'd heard a good deal about being mindful and attended a workshop where the teacher instructed him to first of all learn to sit still and quiet, watch his own breath and learn to understand how his mind worked. The man reported that if he sat still, he soon became bored because he was used to doing things all the time and he was one of those people that gets bored easily!

We all chat, listen to music, watch TV, read a book and do anything to keep ourselves busy, to avoid being bored! Being mindful is about learning to focus on one thing at a time – to calm our mind and concentrate rather than have our thoughts jump from one thing to another.

The teacher emphasised that a good way to calm the mind was to count the breath for, say, twenty minutes.

The man tried this each day for a week and decided to go back to the teacher. "Master, I am so bored watching my breath. Just in and out, in and out. I think I need to work with something more interesting."

"I agree," replied the master, "come with me."

The master led the student to the river and told the man to lean over the bank and watch the water flowing carefully. The man was kneeling down on the bank watching the water intently when the master suddenly grabbed hold of him and held his head under the water until he began to struggle. As he was released, sputtering and struggling to get his breath, the master gently asked, "Now are you bored with your breath?"

Of course, I am not suggesting such a harsh course of action but it is really boring sitting still watching your own breath. Being bored is not a real situation, it's a state of mind and, just as no other person can make you angry, no one can make you feel bored! These are feelings we choose to have in certain situations and just as we should learn to not be angry, we can learn not to be bored when we sit still and quiet.

87 ELEPHANT ROPE

Whilst on holiday in South East Asia, a man visited an elephant work camp deep in the forest. The elephants were used to help logging in the forest to remove excess trees. This stopped overcrowding and provided villagers with building materials to make their homes. The elephant keepers took great care of the animals as they were so valuable to the people who lived in the area.

The visitor was intrigued to see at night each elephant had a small rope tied round one of its hind legs and this was tied to a tree trunk. None of the animals made any attempt to escape. He asked the keeper if it was special rope that was hard to break. The keeper gave a short length of the rope to one of the animals to hold in its trunk, the other end he tied to a tree. On his command the elephant pulled and the rope immediately snapped in two. The man was amazed and realised that if they wanted to, the elephants could pull themselves free and go off into the jungle.

He asked the keeper what was the secret of the animals not escaping.

"First, we take good care of them. We feed them plenty of food, wash them every day and make sure they are not overworked, so they like living here. Also, we bring only orphaned baby elephants here when they are very young and from that early age, we make sure they don't wander off by tying their leg to a tree. At a young age they couldn't break the rope and over time they become conditioned and believe that escape is impossible. Thus, when fully grown and quite able to break the rope as if it was string, they never try!"

What, of course, is true in so many ways is that we become conditioned. We might think ourselves a failure because we have never been very successful, or we might label ourselves as useless or unskilled. These are conditionings. We believe we will always be a certain way because we have been that way for a long time. Plenty of people leave school with few qualifications and many condition themselves to believe they are no good at learning, but this conditioning can be changed. What, how and who you are now is a product of conditioning – so use the time you have to look at your conditionings and if necessary, change them. If the keeper showed the adult elephants how easy it is to pull their leg free, they would, and could, all go off!

88 GOLD COINS

One afternoon, a man sat at the side of the road, head in hands, saddened by his plight. He had no money, nowhere to live and hadn't eaten for four days. He'd fallen out with his family months ago and was too proud to apologise and seek their forgiveness. He'd slept in a barn for the past three nights. He found it difficult to accept his plight and was crying out.

His wailing was heard by a passer-by. The man passing by was very wealthy and always tried to help others when he could; just as he had been helped when he was poor himself.

"Friend, I was once down on my luck as you are and I will help you. I have with me a bag of gold coins and I will give some to you. What will you collect them in?"

The poor man held out a plastic bag.

Before pouring gold coins into the bag, the rich man said, "I will give you gold coins till you say 'enough', but on one condition."

"Okay, what is the condition?" the man asked.

"Should one coin fall to the ground, all the coins will turn to dust."

The poor man accepted the condition and the other man started to pour gold coins into his bag. The bag began to fill up and the rich man repeated his warning about the coins all turning to dust if one touched the ground. The poor man's eyes lit up to see the coins tumble into his bag, but he didn't notice the seam of the bag was being put under pressure.

"More, pour more," he exclaimed.

The rich man tentatively dropped more coins into the bag, but the poor man cried out again, "More, pour more."

Now, with the weight of the coins, the seam of the bag began to open. The poor man noticed the strain on the bag but didn't say 'enough'.

Eventually the inevitable happened… the bag split and all the coins fell to the ground, immediately turning into dust. Sadly, the poor man's greed led to him getting nothing.

Whatever it is, we should know our limits and avoid being greedy.

89 THE PEBBLES AND DEBT

In a small town, many years ago, a tailor found himself in great debt to a loan-shark. For many years he had struggled to make money. The loan-shark was a very old and lonely man, mainly because he was so greedy and made many people struggle to pay his high interest rates. The old loan shark had desires for the tailor's daughter, so he made him an offer that would completely wipe out the debt he owed him. However, there was a catch... he would only wipe out the debt if he could marry the tailor's daughter.

The tailor felt he had no choice. The loan-shark said that he would place two pebbles into a bag, one white and one black. The daughter would then have to reach into the bag and pick out a pebble. If it was black, the debt would be wiped out and the loan-shark would then marry her. If it was white, the debt would also be wiped out, but the daughter wouldn't have to marry the loan-shark. The tailor thought he had a chance to clear his debts and a 50% chance his daughter would be spared her fate.

Standing on a pebble-strewn path in the tailor's garden, the loan-shark bent over and picked up two pebbles. The daughter noticed that the old man had picked up two black pebbles and placed them both into the bag. He then asked the daughter to reach into the bag and pick one. This gave the young woman three choices: she could refuse to pick a pebble from the bag, take both pebbles out of the bag and expose the loan-shark for cheating, or pick a pebble knowing it was black and sacrifice herself for her father's freedom.

Instead, she took a pebble from the bag, and before looking at it 'accidentally' dropped it among the other pebbles on the ground. She turned to the loan-shark and said, "Oh, how clumsy of me. Never mind, if you look into the bag for the one that is left, you will be able to tell which pebble I picked."

The pebble left in the bag was obviously black, and seeing as the loan-shark didn't want to be shown up as a cheat, he had to play along as if the pebble the daughter dropped was white, clearing her father's debt and sparing her having to marry the old man.

Remember not to give in to the only options you think you have – see if you can think outside the box for a different and better solution.

90 THE FARMER'S BUTTER

There was a farmer who kept a few cows, grew a few crops and kept chickens on his small holding at the edge of the village. He sold milk, eggs, cheese and butter to other villagers and had a good life. Each day the local baker bought butter from the farmer and one day he decided to weigh the butter to see if he was getting the right amount. It was light in weight, so he decided to check the following day and once again the butter was short a pound.

Each day for a week he weighed the butter and each day it was underweight. He felt angry and cheated by the farmer and sought help from the Duke who ruled over the land. The Duke called the men to his court where he asked the farmer if he was using any measure to weigh the butter. The farmer replied, "My Lord, I am not a well-educated man and I don't have a proper measure, but I do have a scale."

"Well, my good man, if you have no proper measures, how can you be sure you are giving the man the right weight of butter, and, by all accounts, you are selling him short and cheating him. Each day this week he reports the butter you sold him was underweight."

"Your Honour, long before the baker started buying butter from me, I have been buying a pound loaf of bread from him as does everyone in the village. Every day the baker brings me a freshly baked loaf. So, when he asked to buy my butter, I used my scale to weigh out his butter and I give him the same weight in butter as he gives me in bread. So, if anyone is cheating, it's the baker."

"Indeed," said the Duke, "and for his cheating ways and for falsely accusing you, each day he will give you free bread as well as giving ten loaves each day for a month to the poor of the village."

So, remember you are likely to get as good as you give – act dishonestly, rudely and aggressively and don't be surprised if you get it back. And of course, be kind, generous and polite and that will come back to you.

91 THE WEIGHT OF WATER

A teacher stood in front of her class one morning and standing still she picked up a tumbler of water and held it out at arm's length. For a few minutes she said nothing and the students grew intrigued by her actions. Eventually she smiled at the class and the teacher said, "Today's lesson is based upon this tumbler of water."

"Is it glass half full, glass half empty?" called out one of the students.

"No, it's more challenging than that – how heavy is this glass of water I'm holding?"

Students shouted out answers that ranged from eight ounces to a couple of pounds. The teacher asked one of the students to write down the answers on the class whiteboard. There were seventeen different weights given, ranging from eight to thirty-five ounces.

"Well, as far as I am concerned, the absolute weight of the tumbler and water are not important… although it is one pound one ounce. What matters is how long I hold it for. If I hold it for a minute or two, it seems fairly light and easy to do. If I hold it for an hour, its weight will make my arm ache a little and I will begin to feel uncomfortable. If I hold it for the whole day, my arm will likely cramp up, feel completely numb and paralysed, and eventually I will have no choice but to drop the glass to the floor. In each case, the weight of the tumbler doesn't change, but the longer I hold it, the heavier it feels to me."

The students nodded their heads in agreement, as she continued, "Your stresses and worries in life are very much like the tumbler of water. Think about them for a while and nothing much happens. Think about those stresses and worries for an hour or so and you will begin to ache and feel decidedly uncomfortable. Think about them all day long and you will feel completely numb and paralysed – incapable of doing anything else."

It's important to remember to let go of your stresses and worries. No matter what happens during the day, as early in the evening as you can, put those burdens down. Learn to let go. Don't carry them through the night and into the next day or indeed into the rest of your life. If you still feel the weight of yesterday's stress, it's a strong sign that it's time to put that tumbler down. Hold onto stress and worry too long and it will cause major damage to your health and well-being.

92 THE EXAM

One evening, four university students who shared a house decided to have a night out instead of studying for an important exam. They had too much to drink, went to a club and eventually got home at five in the morning, very drunk. After only three hours sleep, at eight in the morning, one of them woke up and roused the others and reminded them they had to get into university.

As they got up and got ready, one of them said, "Look, we are going to struggle with today's examination, but I have an idea."

They went into the university campus to the lecturer's office and knocked on the door. They apologised for disturbing the lecturer and told him they had been out the evening before for a drive in the country and one of the car tyres picked up a nail and was punctured. They told him they had to walk to a nearby farm to borrow a jack and wheel brace to remove the wheel, only to find they had no spare tyre in the car. Two of them had walked into the town three miles away and found a garage that repaired the tyre. By the time they got back to the car it was after ten o'clock and it was after one in the morning before they got back to their rooms. They had to take the tools back to farmhouse. They said they had not been able to study as they had hoped to and had only slept a few hours. The lecturer said that given the difficulties they had experienced they could take the test in three days' time.

The students went home and spent the three days studying hard to ensure they all passed the examination. On the morning of the exam, they presented themselves at the lecturer's room. He told them he would have to split them up to make sure they only presented their own work, so, each student sat in a room on their own. Each student had an envelope on their desk together with a pad of paper. On the desk was an instruction sheet that said, 'Open the envelope at 09.15 and complete the questions. You have one hour.'

When each student opened their envelope, each contained the same two questions: one, what is your name, two, which tyre got the puncture?

Obviously, the lecturer suspected they were lying and as is often the case, lying is not the best policy as all too often you will be found out. Lies are often impossible to believe and in telling the account you forget details or get the story wrong in retelling. Most of us struggle to remember things that happen, and find it much more difficult to remember lies!

93 SWEETS AND MARBLES

Two children were playing one day in the garden. They were having a great time enjoying the sunshine and each other's company. They lived next door to each other, had started school together and had recently had their tenth birthdays. The boy showed the girl his collection of beautiful, unique marbles and, in turn, the girl showed the boy a box of American Jelly Beans her uncle had brought back for her from his holiday.

The marbles had been collected over time and were of many different sizes and colours. They looked like a bag of jewels to the girl. She might never play with them as marbles but would keep them as objects of beauty.

The beans were not like the ones you could get in local shops and were of many different flavours, many that the boy had never tasted before. He was desperate to own them and boast to his friends that he had real American candy. He would be able to tell his friends that he had sweets that none of them had ever seen, let alone tasted.

The boy suggested that they should do a swap. He would give her all of his marbles if she handed over all of her beans. The girl thought the marbles were beautiful and would last longer than the sweets, so she agreed. The boy handed over his marbles, but kept a couple, the most beautiful ones in his pocket. The girl kept her promise and gave the boy all of her beans.

That night, the girl was happy with the exchange and peacefully went to sleep. The boy, however, could not sleep, as he was up wondering if the girl had secretly kept some of her sweets, just like he did with the marbles.

If you don't give 100% in your relationships, you will always assume your partner isn't giving 100% either. If you want your relationships to be built on trust, you have to be someone who can be trusted 100%. By being honest in relationships, you are holding your partner to do the same. Being completely honest allows you both to be relaxed and confident in the relationship. Being dishonest sets out worries and fears that will make you feel unsettled and uneasy.

94 THE THREE SONS

There was once a man who lived with his three sons and together the four men ran a big department store. His sons were hard workers, but they constantly fought with each other. Even though the man continuously tried to help his sons make peace with each other, he was never successful. In fact, their fighting got to a point where their neighbours made fun of them.

Eventually, the father became ill. He begged his sons to learn how to work together because of his impending death, but they didn't listen. The father feared that after he died, the sons would fight and the business would collapse. So, he decided to teach his sons a practical lesson to help them forget their differences and become a united team.

The father called his sons and said, "I'll give you each an equal collection of sticks to break in half. Whoever breaks the sticks the fastest will be rewarded."

After agreeing to the task, the father gave each of his sons ten sticks and instructed them to break each stick in half. This task took the sons mere minutes to complete, but once they were finished, they started to fight about who finished first.

The father said, "Dear sons, the task isn't finished. Now I'll give each of you ten more sticks. However, you must break the sticks in half as a bundle rather than snapping each one separately." His sons agreed and attempted to do what he had asked. They each tried their best, but none could break the bundle in half. They told their father that they had failed.

In response, their father said, "See, it was easy to break the sticks in half individually, but you couldn't break all ten of them at the same time. Similarly, if the three of you stay united as a team, nobody will be able to harm you. However, if you fight all the time, anyone will be able to defeat you. Please come together as a united team."

This lesson helped the man's sons understand the power of being a team and they promised their father that, moving forward, they would work together as a team, no matter what the situation was.

Being an effective member of a team helps contribute to the overall morale and motivation of the team. Strong teams are made up of individuals who work together, who support each other and cooperate to achieve a mutual goal. Individuals each have different talents, strengths and weaknesses that they bring to the team. If together they stay focused on the task at hand rather than allowing personal disputes to get in the way, they will achieve their desired results.

95 WHERE'S YOUR FURNITURE?

A wise and noble teacher was on a teaching tour that involved visiting thirteen different towns to give a talk and answer questions. He planned each stop so that he could walk up to twenty miles each day to get to the next stop. The last talk was back at his own home town and after two weeks of travel and talking he was looking forward to getting home.

On that last day, he was accompanied by a small group of followers who had brought food to share with the teacher after the talk. The teacher said as they were so near to his home, they should go there to enjoy the food inside his home as the day was very hot and dusty.

The group arrived at the teacher's home and were surprised to see how it was furnished. He told them to put their coats in a small room at the back of the house where there was a small threadbare mat on the floor and one small cushion that they assumed was his bed. The main room had a few small cushions, a rug on the floor and nothing else. The small kitchen had a small stove, one pot, three plates and two spoons in it.

The followers were surprised to see so little in the house and one of them asked the teacher, "Sir, might I humbly ask if you need us to provide you with some furniture and furnishings for your home as you have so little."

The teacher smiled and asked the visitor, "Where is your furniture?"

The man was a little taken back by this and replied, "But sir, I have none, I am only a visitor here."

"So am I," said the teacher.

Maybe this is rather extreme but perhaps we should all look at the things we have around us in our lives. The clothes, shoes, tools, books, furniture and bedding; the list is endless and all of us have more than we will ever need. A friend once told me to write the date in each article of clothing and if when you take it out to wear you realise two years has gone by, give it away, you don't need it! We are all only visiting the earth for eighty or so years and will take nothing with us so maybe we should try and live with less.

96 THE OLD CAR

A father said to his daughter, "You have worked hard at university and graduated with honours, making your mother and I very proud. As a result we are giving you a car that I have stored in a barn on a local farmer's fields. I bought the car the year you were born so it is a vintage model which you should get valued. Hopefully it will give you a boost as you start work. First ask the car sales chap in the village what he will give you for the car."

The daughter went to the used car sales and returned to her father saying, "They offered me £250 because they said it was in a poor condition and would need a lot of work."

The father then said, "Go online to an auction website and see what they will offer."

The daughter went online to several sites, each time putting in the details and number plate. She returned to her father and said, "The best offer I got was £1500, mainly because of its age and because it needs renovation."

The father asked his daughter to go to a car club website and advertise the car with a few pictures. The daughter posted the details on the club website and an hour later she had received six telephone calls, all wanting to buy the car. She came back to her father very excited. "I have had five offers, all over £25,000 for the car. It's a much sought-after collectors' car. A chap is coming today and will pay cash… £38,000!"

Her father said to his daughter, "Remember, the right place and right people will value you the right way. If you are not valued, do not be angry, it means you are in the wrong place; seek those who know your value and those who appreciate you. Never stay in a place where no one sees your true value. You are off into the world of work and need to make sure you are valued – a company might try and get you to work for them cheaply. Remember you have worked hard at university and are a very valuable asset."

Three months later, she started work for a top company on a good salary with excellent work conditions and she drove herself to work in the car she bought from selling the gift her parents gave her.

97 MOVE THE MUG

Tom sat at a table having a cup of coffee with a group of friends when one declared his god was all powerful, that he created the universe and everything in it and there was nothing he could not do.

A second friend chipped in that his god was the master of all and everything and all that happened did so because his god willed it.

A third friend asked how they could both be right and suggested surely one of them must be wrong.

Another said she found it interesting that many religions claim a supreme being that could do everything and who commanded the world. She turned to the group and said, "If there is a god that is all powerful – get him to move my coffee mug across this table."

No one in the group responded to her challenge so she leant forward and moved it herself. "There, even I can move a mug if I put my mind to it, and I am a mere human. Whether there is a god or not, and whoever has the right god, as humans we all have choices. I chose to move the mug and in all my life I can and do make choices and I have to accept the consequences of my actions. If I push the mug too far, it will fall off the table, and I will have to pay for the broken mug and clean up the mess. As is true in my life – if I do good things, good will come to me and if I don't, I will suffer! Whether there is a god is less important than what I must do is be skilful and wise or I will suffer. A god, teacher or wise person might guide me but, in the end, it is by my actions that I will thrive or not. And if there is a god, he will be pleased that I have chosen to be skilful."

98 THE SCISSORS AND THE AXE

One afternoon a young girl turned to her friend in the school playground and said, "You're useless. You can't even skip."

Another girl turned to them both and said, "We cannot all be good at everything. No one and nothing is good at everything."

"Some things are good at everything… scissors are always good at cutting," said the first girl.

"That's true but you couldn't cut down a tree with a pair of scissors. An axe is good at cutting down trees but useless if you wanted to cut your hair or cut out something from a sheet of paper."

"That's true," said the first girl.

The three girls carried on talking about it as they went back into class and the teacher asked them what was so interesting to them that kept them busy chatting. The girls told her and she carefully tore a large sheet of paper into small pieces and gave each student a piece, asking them to write on it five things that they could do.

The children wrote lots of different things: tie shoelaces, play the violin, ride a bicycle, cook an omelette, knit, whistle, skim a stone on a pond, make and fly a kite, juggle, ride a unicycle, swim, bake a cake, fix a puncture on a bike. The children were then asked to go round the class to all the other twenty eight children and see if they could find a classmate who had written the same five things. The class soon became frantically busy as children sought to find a match for their five things.

Eventually a child shouted out, "Miss, it's impossible, no one has the same five as anyone else."

"Then please go back to your own seat," said the teacher. "Indeed, no one has found a match to all their five things! So, remember, like the scissors that can cut hair or paper but cannot cut down a tree, and the axe that can cut down a tree but cannot cut hair or paper, we each have our individual skills that are different from other peoples'."

Scissors are only better than axes for certain purposes. Like all of us, they are good at different things. We are all unique. The only time you should look down on someone is if you want to see what shoes they are wearing.

99 THE NEXT LIFE

A man died and found himself in a splendid place where the scenery was delightful and the air was warm and full of the fragrance of blossom. He was approached by a lady in a pale blue gown.

She said, "Welcome to our abode. I'm here to make sure you have everything you want. You can call me at any time by clapping your hands three times."

The man was most impressed and over the days he established he could have all and anything he wanted to eat, a beautiful home, a wonderful companion, and the car and boat of his dreams. Everything he had ever dreamt about owning on Earth were now his and he wanted for nothing, until one day he clapped his hands and his attendant arrived.

"Please don't think I'm unappreciative and ungrateful but there is something else I would like."

"Speak up. As they say, your wish is my command," she replied.

"Well, I have to say, I am very grateful for everything but there is something I would like."

"Well, what is it?" the lady asked.

"The trouble is I'm a bit bored. I would like a job or at least something to do."

"I'm sorry, Sire, that's the one thing I cannot offer you, there is no work here for you or anyone."

"Well, if that's the case. I might as well be in hell," blurted the man.

The lady turned to him and said quietly, "Where do you think you are?"

We all have things we would wish for, and it is suggested in many places that one of the most important things we need is a sense of purpose, something to do, a job.

100 THE MEN AT LUNCH

Three men had lived in the same small village for a number of years and often greeted each other in the streets around the market. One afternoon, one of the men bumped into the other two as they walked along a street near his home and, realising he barely knew them, he decided he should make a move and try to get better acquainted.

"Friends, we have only exchanged greetings over the years. Maybe we should try and get to know each other better so please come and have lunch with me tomorrow."

The two men came to his house the following day, where he had prepared a simple meal of bread, apples and a few roasted vegetables. The three mean ate and chatted together and got to know each other better.

Lunchtime was coming to an end when one of the men said, "I am enjoying your hospitality and thank you, but I will invite you to my house next week where we will feast on roasted meats of all kinds, the best wine and fruit brought from far off lands that my master, the emperor, provides for me. If only you learnt to flatter the emperor and praise him, you would not have to eat such simple food!"

The other man was surprised to hear his host being put down in such a manner and was about to defend him when the host spoke. "If, my friend, you could learn to be happy with less and to eat simply, you would not need to grovel and demean yourself to the emperor!"

The three men shook hands and parted and vowed to repeat the activity soon.

Think how much easier our own lives would be if we decided to be more humble, less demanding and were prepared to live and eat simply.

101 THE CHESS GAME

A young man approached a wise teacher telling him he was disappointed in his life so far. His father was rich, he had never needed to work and despite all the things, he had never felt satisfied or fulfilled. When he saw the followers of the teacher, he was envious of their serenity and calm and he wanted to feel like that.

The teacher asked the young man what interested him most and he replied that playing chess was what gave him most pleasure. The teacher called for one of his followers, a very elderly woman, and told her to bring a chess board and pieces plus a large sword!

"You will play each other at chess and, old woman, if you lose, I will cut off your head and you will go directly to heaven and, young man, if you lose, I will cut off your head and your suffering will end."

The game started and the young man soon found himself under great pressure as the lady launched an attack on his pieces. He found himself running with sweat as he feared he would lose the game. However, after making a mistake in her moves, the young man found himself in a commanding position, moved in to finish her off and claim victory.

As he did, he looked at her and was taken aback by her calm and serene look. He realised a life of study and wise choices had led to her being very much at peace with whatever happened. He was awash with compassion for the lady, realising his victory would lead to her paying the ultimate price. So, he deliberately made a number of errors until it was her pieces that were poised for victory and it would be his head that would fall.

At that point, the teacher leant forward and tipped the board over, declaring, "There is no winner and no loser. Young man, you have learnt things today that will change your life forever and bring you the satisfaction and peace you desire. You learnt in the game that to succeed you must concentrate on the task in hand and that you must lead your life with compassion for others. Stay with us here for a few weeks and train your heart further to these two tasks and you will return to the world with renewed purpose and joy."

Like all of us, there are only two things we should focus upon in our lives… doing what we are doing as best we can, and doing it with compassion for everything including ourselves.